Geoff was born in Ipswich, Suffolk, and was educated at Langley School in Norfolk. He then studied education and music at Bishop Lonsdale College in Derby and subsequently attained a Bachelor of Education (Honours) degree at the University of Surrey. In July 2022, Geoff was awarded an Honorary Bachelor of Teaching degree at the University of Nottingham.

Geoff is a qualified teacher with over 38 years' experience, twenty-one of which were as a headmaster of two different schools – St Andrew's and St Mark's School in the Royal Borough of Kingston and Collingwood School in the London Borough of Sutton. For a number of years, Geoff was a governor at Langley School – the public school he attended as a boy – and is currently Vice Chair of Governors at St Lawrence C of E Primary School in Chobham, Surrey.

Geoff is also a keen musician and currently sings with the Guildford Choral Society. During his long career, he has been a church director of music, conducted secular choirs and orchestras and was, for thirty years, an honorary local representative of the Associated Board of the Royal Schools of Music.

After his retirement in 2009, Geoff started work as a voice artist (recording radio ads and audio books) and has appeared in a number of films and TV series as a supporting actor. He is now adding published author to his CV!

Geoff is married with three grown up daughters and four beautiful granddaughters.

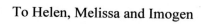
To Helen, Melissa and Imogen

Geoff Barham

FOR HEAVEN'S SAKE

AUSTIN MACAULEY PUBLISHERS™

LONDON • CAMBRIDGE • NEW YORK • SHARJAH

A CIP catalogue record for this title is available from the British Library.

ISBN 9781398404717 (Paperback)
ISBN 9781398416796 (ePub e-book)

www.austinmacauley.com

First Published 2022
Austin Macauley Publishers Ltd®
1 Canada Square
Canary Wharf
London
E14 5AA

I am indebted to my wife, Rosalind, and my daughters, Helen, Melissa and Imogen, who have all given me huge amounts of encouragement, advice and assistance throughout the composition of this book.

Chapter 1

Lost Keys

Father Cyril paused for a moment at the Rectory Gate. His portly frame cut a striking silhouette against the red evening sky and his excessive weight caused him to be breathless even when walking the twenty yards down the garden path.

There was snow on the ground and the Norfolk village of Forling Down was looking particularly picturesque in its wintry guise. It was the first Tuesday in January and Father Cyril had reluctantly ventured out into the Christmas card scene to say Evening Prayer at the Parish Church of St Jude, all of fifty yards from the Rectory. Cyril leant against the gate, wheezing gently. He would far rather be wedged tightly in his favourite armchair in front of a roaring log fire with a glass of vintage port and some of the fine mature Stilton which the Parochial Church Council (PCC) had given him the previous week in his Christmas stocking!

All of a sudden, the geese on the village green became very agitated. Cyril peered over his thin round spectacles and noticed old Ned Gaskin, a retired farm worker and part-time verger at St Jude's, making slightly unsteady progress towards the church.

"Drunk again, Ned," chided Cyril.

"So am oi, Sir," quipped Ned. "Mrs Bloomfield-Upton gave me a splendid lunch and we enjoyed some of 'er Beaujolais Nouveau!"

"Two or three bottles by the look of you," said Cyril disapprovingly. "Once you have rung the bell, if you can locate the rope in your present condition, I think you'd better go straight home to have a cold shower. I don't want you burping all the way through Evening Prayer!"

"Orl roit!" sighed Ned in his broad Norfolk drawl. "Oyll sober up afore the council meetin' tonoit."

Father Cyril leaned even more heavily on the gate. He had forgotten about the PCC meeting that evening and was not at all happy at being reminded. Cyril found most church meetings excessively tedious and much preferred making all the important decisions himself without having to listen to the likes of Colonel Wagstaff and Mrs Bloomfield-Upton, pontificating about church matters which should, he believed, really just be left to the parish priest!

The tranquility of the village was then further disturbed by the cheeky sound of a high-pitched bicycle bell. Into sight came the willowy figure of young Father Aubrey, the rather naive and accident-prone curate.

"What ho, Rector!" he squealed. "Jolly good fun this snow, isn't it?"

Cyril grunted and gained little consolation from the sight of Aubrey skidding headlong into the lychgate at the entrance to the churchyard.

"Bloody fool!" shouted Cyril. "I must have been very wicked in a previous life to have deserved you! Pick yourself up and check that Ned hasn't flown up the church tower on the end of the bell rope – he's a trifle inebriated!"

"Oh right ho!" yelled Aubrey somewhat bruised and covered in wet snow. "See you in a jiff!" Aubrey scooted up the slippery church path on one pedal and skidded to a halt in the church porch. Yet again, he seemed to have exasperated the Rector but this was such a frequent occurrence that he quickly erased it from his memory.

Back at the Rectory Gate, Cyril had made a reluctant decision to ease his ample frame across the snowy street and had begun the short trudge towards St. Jude's. Every step seemed increasingly disabling in the deep snow and he was panting heavily by the time he had arrived at the vestry.

"It better be a short service tonight," wheezed Cyril. "I'm cold, I'm tired and I don't like Psalm 104 – it's far too long! I've decided we'll have Psalm 133 instead – it's only got four verses and then I can get back to the Rectory in time for a nice port and Stilton before tonight's meeting."

Aubrey eyed the Rector up and down somewhat bemused.

"Are you permitted to just swap the jolly old psalms whenever the old spirit moves you Rector?" quizzed Aubrey.

Cyril slowly rotated and his cheeks became even redder than usual. He adjusted his spectacles further down his plump little nose and peered scornfully at his irritating young curate.

"I'll change you in a moment!" spluttered Cyril. "Put your surplice on, stop asking ridiculous questions and start processing into the chapel. As usual, I expect there will only be dear simple old Prudence in the congregation!"

The somewhat comical procession of the spherical Rector and the lanky Curate made its way into the small chapel of Our Lady. There was a dank smell not uncommon in country churches, and the white paint as always was peeling from the walls in several places. As predicted, the only parishioner present was Prudence Pots, a simple country girl now in her fifties, who worked part-time at the Manor and spent two mornings a week polishing the church furniture. The clergy took their places and Cyril started to intone the service in his usual pompous style. Father Aubrey leapt up and down at the appropriate moments and the service was indeed over in record time.

"Lovely service tonight, Father," said Prudence warmly.

"Peace be with you!" retorted Cyril dismissively, desperately trying to squeeze past with his books in the vain hope that he might get home sooner rather than later.

"Spiffing to see you again Prud!" said Aubrey. "How about lunch on Sunday?"

Prudence became visibly quite overcome. She patted her hair, touched her cheeks coyly and turned bright pink.

"That would be lovely," gasped Prudence with disbelief. "I've never been invited out before!"

"No, no you silly old thing," replied Aubrey, patronisingly. "What about me coming to your splendid pad for a bite, Prud?"

Prudence became rapidly deflated and was covered in embarrassment and disappointment.

"Er…yes, I suppose so," choked Prudence, quickly trying to regain her composure and desperately searching in her mind for a credible excuse. "Do you like tripe and onions?"

Father Aubrey knew that this was perhaps not going to be quite what he had in mind and fumbled in his cassock pocket for his bright red Old Etonians' diary.

"Oh dear, dear, Prudence – sorry old thing but I've got another invite that day – perhaps another time eh?" With this, he quickly swept out of the chapel and took solace from the sanctuary of the vestry.

"Lock up Aubrey please," blustered Cyril imperiously. "I'm off. See you tonight at eight for the council meeting."

With that, he rolled out of the church as fast as his little legs could carry him, leaving Aubrey with his mouth ajar, as usual not quite sure how to reply.

As Father Cyril trudged back to the Rectory, the snow began to fall more heavily. His distinctive wire rimmed spectacles became completely covered in snow and the lack of hair on his head certainly did not aid insulation! Unbeknown to Cyril, the Rectory cat Beelzebub was, despite the severity of the weather, languishing in the snow just the other side of the Rectory Gate. Cyril's optical efficiency was much-diminished due to the whiteout and thus, as he approached the somnolent furry feline, he tripped headlong over the poor unsuspecting pussy and landed pate first in a pile of mulch which had only been delivered the previous day and was still steaming despite the cold! There was an eerie silence for a few seconds and then the most almighty shout issued from the cleric of St Jude's.

"What the blazes…You ridiculous animal…You messenger from Hell…What on earth possessed you to sleep in such a stupid place in such Arctic conditions? Are you a penguin you brainless moggy?"

Cyril's plight was now considerable. His barrel-like shape made regaining the vertical a very challenging manoeuvre and the prostrate Rector was experiencing no small problem in achieving this! He eventually managed to sit upright, but now realised that the first tragedy of this unfortunate event was the loss of his spectacles. Without them, he could see very little and with the snow falling, vision was not easy anyway. He began rolling backward and forward and realised that his posterior was now completely soaked. Achieving little but exhaustion and frustration as a result of this comic movement, Cyril then decided to roll to his side and try to kneel. He eventually managed this but in doing so, heard an ominous crunching sound. With some considerable difficulty, he fumbled around underneath his knee, only to locate what by touch, were very obviously his shattered spectacles. The Rector's frustration and exhaustion now changed to despair.

"Help...Help...Help!" screamed Cyril, desperately hoping Aubrey might hear him as he left the church.

Meanwhile, back in St Jude's, Aubrey had lost his church keys. He had searched his trousers, his bicycle panniers, his jacket and all over the vestry, but to no avail.

"Flipping bad luck this," muttered Aubrey. "What can a chap do in a situation like this? I suppose I'd better go to see old Porky and admit to misplacing the blessed things – don't suppose I'll be flavour of the month though!"

Aubrey consoled himself with the fact that he 'NEVER' was flavour of the month anyway so it wasn't going to make the blindest bit of difference whether he'd lost the church keys or the Crown Jewels! The Rector would pour scorn on him and chide him mercilessly for his supposed absent-mindedness. Plucking up courage to face the music, Father Aubrey ventured out into the blizzard to be greeted by the distant bleating of the rapidly freezing Father Cyril, still grounded and now totally disorientated!

"That's awfully strange," mused Aubrey, "Sounds like a cross between a sheep and the Rector! Can't be…He's in the Rectory drinking port, lucky chap…Must be one of Colonel Wagstaff's sheep strayed from the Manor."

As Aubrey approached the Rectory Gate, the cries became louder and clearer. Very soon his eyes alighted on the snow-covered form rolling backwards and forwards in the pile of mulch!

"Good Lord Rector – funny time of day to be gardening isn't it?" enquired Aubrey incredulously. "You should be indoors in this weather? Mind you I suppose you have got the insulation though. Ha…Ha…Ha!"

"For heaven's sake, stop making inane remarks, you blithering idiot and help me up! For your information, I am not gardening and I certainly do not feel particularly well insulated! It's Beelzebub's fault, Aubrey, and now I've broken my spectacles."

"That's a bit steep isn't it Rector…blaming the jolly old Devil every time you don't walk in a straight line," quipped Aubrey. "Age shall not weary…"

"Shut up you fool and get me up!" demanded Cyril, "I'm in no mood for a sermon!"

Aubrey carefully assisted in the righting of the disorientated Rector and helped him up the Rectory path. Cyril fumbled in his cassock pocket in an attempt to locate the Rectory key but found only a rather hairy mint and half a tissue! As the minutes ticked past, the light gradually began to fade and it became very obvious that the key must have flown out of his pocket as he cascaded over the unsuspecting cat. Aubrey then broke the news that he too had lost a key, the church one, and so they both sat on the Rectory step to gain strength and hopefully some inspiration.

Just at that moment, they could hear the unmistakable sound of Colonel Wagstaff's Rolls Royce purring down the road from the Manor.

"Quick Aubrey," screamed Father Cyril, "Flag down the Colonel and request his assistance – if we don't get into the Rectory soon, I'll never make the Church Council meeting and my stomach is beginning to rumble too!"

Aubrey scampered down the Rectory path and made extravagant gesticulations at the Colonel. The whole village knew of Aubrey's eccentricities and thus at first the Colonel took little notice and flashed his lights to move the comic curate out of the way. As he moved closer however, it was abundantly clear that these were not the usual nonsensical gestures of which Aubrey was all too commonly prone. Very obviously there was yet another crisis in Aubrey's life but the question was, should he get involved or let him be as usual?

Much to the relief of both Aubrey and Cyril, the Colonel's impressive white Rolls halted and the driver's window slowly lowered.

"What have you managed to louse up this time old boy?" enquired Colonel Wagstaff. "Got a flat tyre again or did Prudence throw a snowball at you?"

The Colonel always gained much enjoyment from teasing Aubrey and this occasion was no different.

"Colonel Wagstaff Sir," said Aubrey, "The Rector is locked out of the Rectory and we can't find the church keys either…in fact the Rector has also taken a nasty tumble. Can you please help us?"

Reluctantly, the Colonel alighted from his centrally heated vehicle and trudged up the Rectory path.

"Thank goodness you're here, Colonel," gasped Cyril. "Can you get your spare key to the Rectory please, and your spare key to the church? I'm freezing, fed up and very hungry."

Colonel Wagstaff found the snow-covered sight of the barrel-shaped Cyril hilarious and began roaring with laughter. When he regained control of his mirth, he helped the shivering, spherical and somewhat embarrassed cleric into the Rectory and sat him down in his favourite chair in front of the fire.

Much relieved that at least one key had been located for the church, Aubrey braved the elements once again and trudged back to St Jude's to lock up. He too wanted some time for a snack before the dreaded PCC meeting later in the evening!

Chapter 2

The PCC Meeting

"What the...........uurh!" Spluttered Cyril who had just discovered a dead woodlouse in his oxtail soup. "It's the last time I buy food from the Mothers' Union stall at the Christmas Fayre!"

Father Cyril had been reduced to a quick TV snack following his unfortunate contretemps with his cat Beelzebub on the Rectory path. He had hoped to watch 'Coronation Street' prior to the dreaded PCC meeting but things as usual were not going at all well. Since being unceremoniously delivered back to the Rectory, the Archdeacon had rung about the quinquennial inspection of the church fabric and had not been at all amused that Cyril had skilfully avoided one for the previous twelve years; Mrs Bunting had called with her dead cat Pussy Galore in an old wine box demanding a burial with full ceremonial honours; and Aubrey had tripped whilst putting out the lights in St Jude's and had fallen against the church bell mechanism causing the fragile chiming device to strike twelve every quarter of an hour much to the extreme annoyance of Mrs Napier whose three year old Hermione could not get to sleep! Now it was ten to eight and Cyril had neither managed to view any of his favourite TV soap nor succeeded in preparing or eating any acceptable supper! Quickly, a relative term as far as Father Cyril was concerned, he wrapped a generous portion of well-matured Stilton in a page of the Church Times and put some port in his frequently used hip flask. He then reluctantly trudged through the now even deeper snow to the room above the Newt and Ferret pub for the meeting of the St Jude's Parochial Church Council, a very bizarre collection of humanity by any standards!

By the time Cyril had negotiated the narrow winding staircase to the upper room, his ruddy complexion was even redder and his breathing sounded very like the Flying Scotsman about to depart from Euston station in days of yore! Mrs Bloomfield-Upton, the PCC Secretary, and the Colonel had already arrived as had Ludevic Pipe, the church organist, who was shortly to be the main focus of uneasy discussion at the meeting. Edwin Jones, the butcher, was nearly asleep at the far end of the table and Priscilla Grindthorpe was poring over a copy of 'The Lady'. Father Aubrey and Rodney Hitcham were as usual discussing life at Eton. They were both trying to outdo the other with a story of some lamentable incident from their school days.

"I think it's time we began," said the exasperated Cyril, having regained some semblance of normal respiratory control. "We have the agenda in front of us and I should like to get to item five before midnight!"

Item five concerned the future of Lu Pipe, as he was affectionately or not so affectionately known, the church organist. He was a rather thin, eccentric individual who always played the same three hymns and 'Air on a G String' as the recessional voluntary. He had thick round-rimmed spectacles, a bushy moustache and was often seen with a pipe in his mouth. The choir had all long-since become fed up and left, all four of them, and the Church Council had been charged with the task of 'doing something or else' at the last Annual General Meeting.

"Are there any apologies for absence Mrs Bloomfield?" asked Cyril impatiently.

"Bloomfield-UPTON," she corrected imperiously.

"Edwin is usually fairly absent-minded," quipped Aubrey, "Jolly short on the old cerebral – just look at him!" Edwin was indeed snoring loudly and showing no signs of consciousness.

Priscilla skilfully extracted her hatpin and sunk it deeply into Edwin's unsuspecting buttock! "Yarooch!" yelled the pained butcher.

"Wake up will you!" demanded Father Cyril. "This is a council meeting not one of Aubrey's sermons!"

"I beg your pardon" said Aubrey indignantly. "I think my jolly old orations are spot on, don't you Rodney?"

"Rather," responded Rodney supportively, "Better than old Bunter's anyway!"

Father Cyril pounded the table with his podgy fist. "Pull yourselves together – we haven't got time for all this nonsense. I must insist that you keep your immature quips to yourself, Aubrey. Now what about the accounts, Priscilla?"

Priscilla Grindthorpe, the PCC Treasurer, worked in the City and was certainly no fool. Father Cyril usually felt quite uneasy in her presence as he could not match her intellectually and had to rely on his status to keep her in check.

"Well," began Priscilla, "We are as usual living beyond our means. The deposit account stands at five hundred and three pounds following the generous Studely-Walker bequest but the current account shows a deficit of three hundred pounds. Furthermore, the bank has written in pretty stern terms demanding, quite rightly, to know when we expect to enjoy a credit balance? Regrettably Father Cyril, I have had to reply, saying that during your incumbency, we are very unlikely to enjoy any such happy monetary state in the foreseeable future."

Cyril's glasses had steamed up and his ruddy face, now extremely red, looked ready to explode.

"Why was I not consulted Miss Grindthorpe? Do you realise that the tone of your letter is a little short of slanderous?"

"Pretty damn truthful though, eh?" interjected Aubrey. "The old account should have a few quid in it, Rector. Not playing ball with the old bank if we continuously drain the jolly old thing down!"

"Shut up Aubrey," bellowed Cyril. "Priscilla, I shall take Chairman's action on this. We must sell the organ! I am now going to move to item five on the agenda – 'The future of the church organist'."

"Rector, I think this is all highly irregular," said Colonel Wagstaff. "I think we need to discuss the church finances in more detail to discover why we are so short of money?"

"Item five," retorted Cyril emphatically. "We must discuss the sale of the organ. It does not work properly and has not been played properly since Mr Pipe arrived. He only knows a few hymns and never uses more than one finger at a time!"

"So few notes work" interrupted Ludevic, "that you only need one finger. As for the repertoire, the hymn books are in such a poor state of repair that we only have the right pages for about three hymns."

"I think the organist has a point there, Rector," drawled Mrs Bloomfield-Upton in her usual rather aristocratic tone. "We require a decent instrument and a proper new set of hymn books."

"Well said!" interjected Aubrey.

"Rather," agreed Rodney.

"No, no, no, no!" said Cyril emphatically. "We have no money for a new organ, no money for new hymn books, and little prospect of increasing revenue with only ten on the electoral roll!"

"A church has stood here in Forling Down for over eight hundred years," began the Colonel who was obviously getting prepared for a lengthy speech. "It is a splendid and vital part of our village life and must be retained at all costs. I fought in two world wars so that England should be free and so that our heritage should be preserved."

"God save the Queen!" shouted Aubrey leaping up!

"And long live the Empire!" retorted Mrs Bloomfield-Upton.

Edwin, who had been nursing his injured right buttock following Priscilla's lunge with the hatpin, was unaware that the conversation had quickly moved on, and inquired why the church accounts were in such a sorry state. Priscilla, who was delighted to return to this vital topic, began, despite protestations from the Rector, to explain that the usual convention when attempting to balance an account was to enjoy some sort of income as well as expenditure!

"Last year," concluded Priscilla beginning to feel in command of all present, "We exceeded our ridiculously modest income by some three hundred pounds."

"Very well," sighed Cyril, becoming more and more exhausted by the proceedings, "What do you suggest?"

The Rector was beginning to show his customary impatience and became particularly bad-tempered when being attacked by pompous females! He lowered his spectacles slightly and peered over them, daring anyone to question his clerical authority.

"What about a horticultural show?" suggested the Colonel.

"Oh yes," gushed Mrs Bloomfield-Upton. "I've got two lovely marrows you can have straight away!"

Rodney Hitcham could not contain his schoolboy immaturity at this last retort and began roaring with laughter uncontrollably!

"I've been fortunate enough to see Mrs Bloomfield-Upton's brill marrows!" quipped Aubrey equally amused. "They're quite something Rector!"

"I fail to understand your mirth, Aubrey, do control yourself please," chided Cyril. "However, the idea of a country show is probably not such a bad one – what do you think Priscilla?"

"Anything that stems the tide of financial decline in Forling Down Parish Church, must be worthy of consideration Rector," said Priscilla, "But who will organise it and where could it be held?"

Cyril cast his eyes around the table and gazed at Colonel Wagstaff. He knew Forling Manor, the Colonel's estate, would be an ideal venue and he certainly did not wish it to be held in the Rectory garden. That would involve far too much effort and was to be avoided at all costs.

"How about it Colonel?" enquired Cyril. "Can we hold it at the Manor – it's the obvious place?"

"Probably be OK old chap," said the Colonel, "But it mustn't clash with the Forling Hunt though – I'll check out a few dates in the morning."

"Splendid," wheezed Cyril, much relieved. "Now please may we consider the thorny matter of the church organ? You will recall that the Annual General Meeting charged us with doing something to improve the music, and at the moment we have a 'pipe' problem both inside and in front of the instrument."

"Well really Rector – I think that's a bit below the belt! I'd like to hear you do better," squeaked the pear-shaped organist! "How can I be expected to achieve anything on an instrument that hasn't been tuned or serviced since the Reformation, and I might say, with no choir."

"May I remind you, Mr Pipe," began the Rector, "That there was a choir prior to your arrival and it was only when they discovered your complete lack of musical ability that they decided to find pastures new."

"Well really," exploded Lou, "I may not be Sir David Willcocks but I have played on some of the largest organs in Britain and have been involved in church music for decades. Give me a decent instrument and some humanity with just a small modicum of musical sense and I could work miracles."

Aubrey and Rodney were convulsed uncontrollably in the corner and each time Lu mentioned 'organs', hooted even more loudly! "It'll take a greater miracle than the changing of water into wine to expect acceptable music at St

Jude's whilst you are seated on that organ," chided Mrs Bloomfield-Upton imperiously.

Aubrey and Rodney roared even more loudly and were only outdone in terms of decibels by the continuous snoring of Edwin! "This is hopeless," sighed Cyril. "I am surrounded by incompetence, schoolboy hysterics, a comatose butcher, insults and the imperious chidings of various feuding upper class pomposity. The business of the church music will obviously have to be deferred until some form of sanity returns to Forling Down – now let us finish with the Grace."

"Oh, is it time to eat?" chirped Edwin who had just regained consciousness!

"Shut up you fool," exploded Cyril. "May the Grace of our Lord Jesus.........Amen."

"Amen," agreed all present as the chaotic meeting broke up.

Cyril eased his frame down the difficult staircase once more and fought through the blizzard conditions to once again regain the solace of his comfortable armchair in front of a welcoming log fire, still with a few embers flickering. "Where's that Port and Stilton?" he wheezed. "I need something to calm my nerves before I go to bed." He poured himself a large glass of his favourite vintage port, cut a generous slab of Stilton and sank into his chair exhausted.

"Ah," he murmured contentedly, "Utopia at last!"

Chapter 3
Aubrey Goes Climbing

Aubrey woke early as usual the next day and leapt out of bed like a frightened gazelle! He flung wide the curtains which revealed a very white snowy scene, turned sharply, tripped over the vacuum cleaner carelessly left out the previous day, and cascaded head over heels into an airer of washing at the opposite end of the room. Somewhat dazed, he arose from the pile of clothes hilariously sporting home-produced Catholic boxer shorts with a picture of the Pope on the reverse! The latter had been a gift from Rodney Hitcham the previous year and caused some consternation when shown at the Mother's Union tea party prior to being worn!

"What a sight!" sighed Aubrey looking at himself in the mirror. "If the rest of the day continues like this, I fear the worst!"

Extricating himself from his errant underwear, he stumbled into the bathroom in a bid to commence his early morning ablutions. He turned on the tap which came off in his hand, splashed icy cold water on his face in a vain attempt to wake himself up properly, and fumbled for the toothpaste.

"Drat," he yelped, squirting a jet of the white and red striped mixture into his left eye by mistake. "Why the jolly old blazes can't a chap be spared all this hassle so early in the morning? Perhaps I should return to the horizontal and try again!"

Once downstairs, the day did not proceed much better. Aubrey attempted to make some tea but dropped the tea caddie on the floor spraying tea leaves everywhere'. He then opened the fridge to procure some milk only to knock over a container of spaghetti hoops which landed fair and square on his left foot. Next he managed to slip on a carelessly discarded duster, and proceeded to fall headlong into the cat's breakfast of tripe! Aubrey by this time had had quite enough and it was rapidly approaching the time when he should be appearing at St Jude's for the early eight o'clock service. Cyril would castigate him unmercifully if he was late and Aubrey was earnestly praying that the day was going to improve and not get worse!

He quickly donned his black cloak and green Wellingtons and trudged slowly across the road towards the village church.

All seems very quiet, thought Aubrey, glancing at his watch. "Where's dear old Porky? He's usually here by now – it's almost ten to eight."

Certainly the church was firmly locked and, to be sure, there was no sign of life anywhere. It had started to snow a light, wispy snow and the village was absolutely still. Aubrey resolved to make his way to the Rectory to see if the Rector was en route and trudged through the now rather heavier snowfall and up the Rectory path. He knocked on the thick oak door and awaited a response from Father Cyril.

None was forthcoming. Aubrey looked at his watch again and observed that it was now five to eight.

"I must do something," he muttered, "the coach loads of jolly old parishioners will be winging their way to the old eight o'clock service any minute now and at the moment their entry to the church is most surely barred!"

Aubrey plunged his right hand into the cold white snow and managed to locate a cold moist stone from the path. He carefully aimed it at Cyril's window and like David before Goliath, let the missile fly. A microsecond later there was a shattering sound and the top left pane in the Dickensian style window fell onto the Rectory path. Aubrey by this time had already begun saying more prayers and felt sure his time as curate at St Jude's might well be terminated quite soon! Despite this inadvertent indiscretion, there was still no sign of life at the Rectory and Aubrey determined to try one more ploy. Noticing an ancient black drainpipe which conveniently rose from the left of the front door right past Cyril's bedroom window, Aubrey started preparing himself for a risky manoeuvre. He first clambered onto the rainwater butt and then hauled himself upwards a little at a time. The pipe was extremely cold, moist and old, and Aubrey was by no means convinced that it would stand the strain. It had certainly not been designed as a climbing aid for desperate curates and the whole escapade brought back painful memories of a foolish prank at Eton involving him and several other boys. This had resulted in the whole group receiving a caning from the livid house master! Now about six foot off the ground, Aubrey dared not look down. His hands fumbled for suitable spaces between the pipe and the brickwork and were becoming more and more numb as each second passed. He was now within a couple of feet of Cyril's bedroom window and he made one last Herculean effort to haul himself up to the ledge. He paused, frozen and exhausted, and heard the chimes of St Jude's announce that it was eight o' clock. Simultaneously, the front door of the Rectory creaked open and a bespectacled Rector peered out, obviously suffering from an excess of Port the previous evening and considerable displeasure at having to rise so early. He moved into the cold and snow and began shuffling down the Rectory path. As his feet slowly trudged through the ever-deepening snow, there was a crunching sound which even to Cyril in his somewhat glazed early morning state did not resemble the sound of leather on soft newly laid snow. His rounded head glanced down and there sparkling in the early morning light was glass!

"Ruddy louts – another of their discarded beer bottles I suppose" chided Cyril, but as he walked on, he noticed yet more and looked more closely.

Aubrey at this moment turned and looked down dislodging an old bird's nest as he did so. The nest tumbled earthwards bouncing off Cyril's head as it did so.

"What the blazes was that?" yelped the Rector in shock. He cast his eyes upwards towards his bedroom window and they eventually alighted on his shaking, frozen curate peering like some medieval gargoyle from the side of his bedroom window.

"What the bloody hell are you doing up there Aubrey? Have you taken complete leave of your senses you ridiculous fool? This is no time for mountaineering practice – you should be preparing for the Eucharist. Are you under some misguided illusion that you are nearer to your Lord up my drainpipe, because I can assure you that you may well meet Him earlier than you thought! And perhaps you would care to venture an opinion as to how glass from my bedroom window should now be underneath my left foot?"

"I can explain everything, Rector," spluttered Aubrey who by now was almost completely numb and beyond caring. "I was trying to attract your attention, Rector..."

"Ever heard of a door knocker you idiot?" interrupted Cyril. "Didn't they teach you anything at that posh public school of yours? Door knocker...d...o...o...r k...n...o...c...k...e...r placed on doors, for the use of humans, in order to attract the attention of those inside!" roared Cyril becoming redder by the second.

"I tried everything Rector, including throwing a flipping stone at your window but I couldn't attract your attention – I was worried that the church would not be open for the eight o'clock service," pleaded Aubrey.

"Bloody fool!" muttered Cyril in total exasperation. "Come down immediately and stop behaving like a complete delinquent. When I agreed to take on a curate, much against my better judgement, I did not expect to receive a neurotic orangutan who would be shinning up drainpipes before breakfast every morning! I shall suggest to the Bishop that he provides me with a large supply of valium and you with some strychnine. I am a firm believer in the principle of euthanasia for curates!"

Aubrey tried to move but was far too cold and now completely petrified on two counts. Firstly he was suffering more and more from a debilitating bout of vertigo and secondly he did not relish the prospect of a face to face encounter with Father Cyril who was certainly not displaying any semblance of priestly forgiveness at the present time!

"I can't move," croaked Aubrey wishing that the day had never started. "Please help me, Rector – I'm petrified."

Cyril could see that Aubrey was now in a pretty desperate situation and a modicum of compassion began to seep into his veins.

"Stay there for a moment while I let Prudence know that today's service is off and I'll get the Colonel to send a ladder down with old Ned," yelled Cyril as he marched across the snow-covered street towards St Jude's.

"I don't think I shall be moving very far in my current old state Rector," whispered Aubrey with very little voice left at all. "Please hurry though – my jolly old feet are like ice cubes and I haven't had any sensation in my hands for at least half an hour!"

Cyril duly informed simple Prudence who was the only member of the St Jude's congregation who ever attended the weekday eight o'clock services. She then followed Cyril back to the Rectory giggling that she'd never seen Aubrey stuck up a ladder before!

"Cooee, Father Aubrey!" shrieked Prudence. "What are you doing up a drainpipe dear?"

"Cooee, to you!" choked an embarrassed Aubrey. "We've had a little mishap and I need a ladder!"

"Problem with your bladder did you say?" enquired Prudence not renowned for her powers of hearing or concentration. "Shall I fetch a chamber pot?"

"Not BLADDER Prudence old thing, LADDER ...L...A...D...D...E...R...I need a ladder," said Aubrey desperately.

"Oh I've got one of those in my stockings," chirped Prudence trying to keep up some sort of polite conversation. "Would you like to see it?"

"Not just now Prudence," croaked Aubrey quickly. "Please help the Rector obtain a ladder!"

Meanwhile, inside the Rectory, Cyril had phoned Forling Manor and Ned had been despatched with the desperately needed ladder. The Colonel had roared with laughter when he heard of Aubrey's plight and had invited the two of them to dinner that evening in order to plan the prospective horticultural show. He hoped Aubrey would be suitably recovered in time!

Ned duly arrived with the ladder a few moments later, Aubrey was safely returned to the ground and Prudence scuttled back to her cottage still giggling at the sight of their local curate stuck up a drain pipe!

Cyril retired into the Rectory, placed an old hymn book in front of the broken window pane, and then relaxed downstairs in front of a newly laid log fire with a hot cup of Irish coffee.

"Ah," he sighed, "this is more like it – a few hours of calm before the next storm!"

Chapter 4

Dinner at the Manor

By early afternoon, the snowfall had begun to ease and there were now only a few wispy flakes still falling on the weighted branches of the trees. A slight breeze began to blow dusty snow off the roof tops and every so often the occasional seagull swooped over St Jude's looking for food.

Cyril had spent the afternoon playing himself at chess and was pleasantly surprised when he discovered that he had won! Aubrey had spent the morning in the bath thawing out and had then retired back to bed where he languished for two and a half hours. He was then abruptly woken by an avalanche of snow crashing down the chimney, producing a large pall of soot dust and fine particles of cement grit. This lingered over the bedroom for what seemed an eternity. The sight of Aubrey trying to sweep up soot wearing only a bath towel was very comical!

"Drat, drat and double drat!" he sighed with exasperation. "Why is it always me that seems to be the recipient of catastrophes?"

Gradually he cleared the worst of the soot from his bedroom floor and decided to return yet again to the bathroom for the third wash of the day! Thankfully this visit passed without incident and by seven thirty that evening, he was ready to go up to the Manor.

Cyril too had begun to trudge the half mile up to the Manor House and was musing about the forthcoming horticultural show. He was then sharply jolted back to reality as Aubrey flew past him shrieking on his bicycle!

"What ho, Rector! Quicker using the old wheels don't you think?" he teased, skidding from side to side in the newly laid snow.

"Look out you blithering idiot, there's a........." At this point Cyril's words were cut short as Aubrey careered headlong into a large snowdrift landing unceremoniously on the opposite side of the road with his head in the hawthorn hedge.

"Oh you beastly snow!" whined Aubrey. "Can't a chap even cycle half a mile without disaster befalling him? Now I'm soaked again! What on earth shall I tell the Colonel?"

"Honesty is always the best policy," barked Cyril imperiously. "Better tell the Colonel that you were riding in inappropriate weather conditions, with little attention to hazards ahead, whilst conducting an inane conversation, and with your head turned round the wrong way! I think that should paint a very clear picture and sum up the situation pretty well."

"Oh really Father!" pleaded Aubrey, "I had hoped you would be able to show a little more sympathy towards your loyal, devoted curate. I've had a positively beastly day so far and I was hoping that this evening was going to pass rather more successfully than the rotten earlier part of the day! I need a little encouragement and understanding, not constant chiding!"

"You need putting down!" interjected Cyril quickly. "Get up you adolescent baboon and wheel that bent old bicycle of yours the last few yards before you make yourself look even more foolish."

Aubrey reluctantly retrieved his buckled bike from the snow-drift and dragged it the last few yards up to the door of Forling Manor. Cyril pulled the impressive chain which duly sounded the bell. Shortly afterwards the door creaked open, and before them, dwarfed by the huge doorway of the medieval Manor House, was the diminutive form of Charity Trussup, the Colonel's housekeeper. Charity was in her sixties and had worked for the Colonel for over forty years. She was timid and painfully shy, but always oozed courtesy and kindness.

"Do come in, Sir," said Charity in her quiet, high-pitched Suffolk drawl. "Oi know the Colonel's expectin' you."

She then noticed the rather bedraggled, wet, shivering curate standing pathetically behind the Rector. He was holding a bent metal frame which sported two rather oval wheels!

"I apologise for Aubrey," sighed Cyril, "I suppose you couldn't find the poor old chap some dry clothes and a towel – he had an argument with a snowdrift on the way up the drive!"

"Yes, of course my dear," responded Charity. "Preps you'd loik ta go inter the drawin' roam, Father, whilst oi troy ta found Father Aubrey some clean clothes. Oi'll tell Colonel Wagstaff that you're 'ere."

Charity sat Aubrey down in the Butler's Pantry and went off to locate some old dry clothes. Meanwhile Aubrey took off his wet boots and began to dry his hair with an old towel that had duly been provided. Soon Charity appeared with a checked sports jacket, some green breeches and some yellow socks!

"Are these any good to ya?" enquired Charity softly. "They were in a bag ready to go to the poor of the parish but oi guess the Colonel won't moind you borrowin' them for an hour or so."

"That's awfully kind, Charity, old thing," answered Aubrey gratefully. "I think I'll look a little bit of a clown in this get-up but I suppose it's better to be dry!"

Charity left Aubrey to change and returned to the Drawing Room where the Colonel was welcoming Father Cyril.

"Ah Charity," called the Colonel imperiously. "Father Cyril would like a sherry."

At this point, Aubrey appeared in the doorway to the Drawing Room looking uncannily like Sir Andrew Aguecheek from Shakespeare's 'Twelfth Night'! The Colonel glanced across the room towards the door, as did Cyril, and both stood transfixed for a second, trying to take in what they saw.

"Good of you to dress for dinner," quipped the Colonel. "Interesting taste in clothes Aubrey – they look a bit like some I used to have a few years ago – do you shop at Harrods too?" Cyril at this point thought he had better offer some brief explanation for Aubrey's somewhat eccentric attire and proceeded to recount the sorry catalogue of events. Aubrey by this time had also been offered a sherry and soon all three were relaxing in front of the large Manor House fire watching the huge logs flickering in the ancient grate. About twenty minutes passed before there was a loud crash on the gong. Charity then reappeared, still vibrating with striker in hand!

"Ah splendid!" announced the Colonel easing himself out of his comfortable chair. "Come on chaps, let's move next door into the Dining Room. What good things have you got for us tonight, Charity? I'm starving!"

All three followed the frail Charity into the Dining Room and took their places at the large baronial table. The Colonel sat at one end, Cyril was instructed to sit at the other and Aubrey sat in the middle. Soon Charity reappeared yet again, this time carrying a tray of hot game soup. She carefully placed a bowl in front of each of the guests and then proceeded to withdraw, walking backwards, nodding subserviently, as she returned to the kitchen.

"Have a hunk of bread with your soup gentlemen? It was baked this morning in the Manor kitchen. I must say it always smells wonderful when Charity is baking."

Both the clerics eagerly agreed to partake of the bread with their soup and were soon thoroughly enjoying the fare. For Aubrey this was the first decent meal for some time and he was certainly appreciating the sumptuous spread. He took a large bite from the beautiful bread and then paused. He looked at his hand and noticed his large replica papal-style ring was missing. It was certainly on a few moments previously as he had observed that it matched the colour of the curtains. Aubrey wracked his brain and took another spoonful of soup. To his horror he spotted that there was something in his bowl. Upon closer scrutiny, it looked uncannily like his missing ring, so he surreptitiously guided the foreign body to the surface of the soup and sure enough there it was. It must have fallen whilst he was hungrily grabbing at the bread. Now he had a dilemma. How was he going to retrieve the valuable ring without appearing to be indelicate?

Aubrey began to weigh up the options. He could dunk his bread in the soup and pull the ring out at the same time? Nobody else seemed to be doing any dunking however so that idea would probably be out. He then considered guiding it onto his spoon, sipping the soup around it, and then accidentally dropping the spoon and ring onto the floor. That would definitely have been a possibility but he would doubtless be accused of being clumsy and bad-mannered yet again, and it would almost certainly create quite a stir. The only other possibility would be to fish in his bowl with his fingers? That would be very obvious however and the others were highly likely to notice his deplorable behaviour? Aubrey, yet again, was presented with a major problem but why, he mused uneasily, did it always happen to him? At that moment, quite by chance, Charity appeared again and as she entered, she tripped on the carpet, dropping a large ornate wine glass on the carpet as she struggled to maintain her composure.

"Charity, those glasses belonged to my uncle, the Earl of Norwich. Do be careful!" exclaimed the Colonel in despair.

As all eyes turned to the floor at Charity's feet, Aubrey seized the moment, fumbled clumsily in the soup for his ring, licked it (and his fingers) and replaced the errant item of jewellery back on his finger. Meanwhile, Charity had burrowed under the table and recovered the glass. Thankfully it was not damaged and she now waited, having dusted herself down, for the Colonel's next instruction.

"I think we've finished with soup, Charity," said Colonel Wagstaff], "but my guests would like some wine. Father Cyril likes a good claret and I dare say Aubrey will have the same, eh Aubrey?"

"Jolly good idea Colonel," agreed Aubrey relieved that the ring incident had now passed unnoticed. "Any wine will do for me!"

"Philistine!" muttered Cyril. "Wines need to be chosen carefully. Just shows how little taste you have? I thought Eton was supposed to be full of socialites from good backgrounds with a degree of breeding? Anyone would think you had been to the local secondary modern!"

"Well what about this horticultural show gentlemen?" asked the Colonel quickly trying to guide the conversation away from the continuing bickering between the two clerics. "Do you still plan to have it at the Manor?"

Cyril explained that the Manor was the obvious place for the show and he would very much like it to be there if at all possible.

"Well the hunt is over by Easter time," said the Colonel, "so if you plan to have it in the summer or early autumn that should be in order."

Charity appeared at this moment carrying huge platters of guinea fowl, closely followed by a number of terrines containing a wide variety of vegetables, Aubrey's eyes were on stalks. He had not enjoyed such a marvellous feast since he'd been invited to Rodney's parents' house the previous year. As the vegetables were passed around, Aubrey certainly didn't stint himself. Cyril too was hungry after his fraught morning and afternoon of chess, so he too filled his plate to excess.

The Colonel lifted his glass and proposed a toast: "To the Forling Down Horticultural show!"

"To the Show!" retorted Cyril and Aubrey in unison, downing the excellent claret together.

The conversation then revolved around the possible ideas for the show and what should and should not be included. Cyril was very keen to have competitions and Aubrey thought some sort of animal section might attract some extra attendance. The Colonel generously offered to arrange a small horse show and some show jumping, and all now began to become really enthusiastic.

"I'll have a quiet word with the key members of the PCC over the next few weeks," said Cyril yawning. He was now becoming very sleepy after his excesses of food and drink. "Once everyone seems to be keen on the ideas, I'll make an announcement in church and we can then formulate more detailed plans."

Offering profuse thanks for some wonderful hospitality, Cyril and Aubrey then reluctantly bid farewell to the Colonel, and Charity produced the curate's soiled clothes neatly folded in a Harrods bag! Aubrey decided to leave the metal sculpture which once passed as his bike by the front door of the Manor. The two clerics trudged rather unsteadily through the now crisper snow under a starlit sky back to their respective residences in the village. All had thoroughly enjoyed the meal and the show was to go ahead as planned. The day had certainly ended much better than it had begun!

Chapter 5

Aubrey's Sermon Doesn't Go to Plan

It was the end of February and the early winter snow had long since melted. As is often the case in Norfolk however, there was a bitter east wind blowing and the village of Forling Down was waking to another very cold day. It was the last Sunday of the month and it had been agreed by the church council that the date of the very special horticultural show should be announced at the morning service that day. The bell on the church tower struck the hour as usual, heralding another new day and in the small terraced curate's cottage at the far end of the village, a light appeared in the upstairs bedroom. Aubrey had had the misfortune to hear the bell but owing to his somnolent state, had failed to count the number of chimes correctly!

"Eight…nine…ten……oh crikey, I'm going to be late for the service and I'm doing the jolly old sermon – old Bunter will be livid!" groaned Aubrey.

'Old Bunter', as Aubrey so irreverently called the Rector, was already up. It was after all half past seven and Father Cyril had the unenviable responsibility of presiding over the eight o'clock service first before having to suffer Aubrey's sermon at the nine thirty! He was enjoying a leisurely cup of tea from his favourite large breakfast mug and listening to the forbidding howls of the wind buffeting the Rectory.

"I shall certainly have to wrap up warm this morning," muttered Cyril trying to put off the evil hour of his departure from the relative warmth of the Rectory.

Meanwhile, Aubrey had flung back the bedclothes in panic and he too heard the howling of the piercing east wind and sensed the sub-zero temperature. He fumbled vainly for the switch on his bedside lamp but only succeeded in knocking over his large old-fashioned alarm clock, his glass of water and the gilt framed picture of his parents at his prize giving at Eton. As the various items plummeted to the floor, he heard simultaneously the breaking of glass, the clattering of metal and the splashing of water.

"Oh bloody hell!" he groaned in sheer frustration. "This is likely to be another one of those days – I feel it in my water!" He stumbled towards the light switch, stubbing his toe on the alarm clock. He eventually managed to illuminate his rather poky bedroom. Not even thinking to check the time, he quickly splashed some icy cold water on his face, squirted a generous centimetre of toothpaste onto his Donald Duck toothbrush, quickly donned his black cassock and scarf, bobble hat and overcoat, and shot out of the door like a bolt from a crossbow, speeding up the road to St Jude's. The wind was indeed biting cold and Aubrey had to fight every step of the way head down, hardly noticing a thing as he went. As he approached the church, squinting to avoid the wind hurting his eyes, he eventually made out the silhouette of the Rector approaching from the Rectory side.

"What the blazes are you doing up so early, Aubrey?" chided Cyril in disbelief. "Couldn't you sleep? Getting nervous about your sermon or have you at long last become additionally devout?"

"I'm sorry, I'm cutting things a trifle fine, Rector," said Aubrey apologetically, thinking that the Rector was in a sarcastic mood. "I'm afraid I dropped the jolly old alarm clock but I won't bore you with all the other irritating details!"

Cyril at this point was quite convinced that Aubrey had flipped completely. He had always known he was eccentric, inept, clumsy, accident prone and unreliable, to mention just a few, but to be wandering around the village pretending to be late for a service was cause for grave concern indeed. Undaunted, he took the confused curate into the vestry, sat him down in front of the clock, and waited. Aubrey blinked twice and then began to focus on the timepiece in front of him. He blinked again and then the dreadful truth dawned. There he was in the church a full hour and a half before he needed to be, and he was cold, confused and not least of all......hungry.

"As you're here," said Cyril, "you can assist me with the eight o'clock service. You will get bonus points for holiness then. You can read the lessons and then I'll take you back to the Rectory for a little breakfast!"

Aubrey could hardly believe his ears. Father Cyril, the personification of unreasonableness, had just invited him to the Rectory for some sort of hospitality. He thought perhaps it was all a ghastly dream, but after he had pinched himself twice, very firmly, he realised that it was indeed for real.

Ah well, he thought to himself, *I ought to make the most of this whilst it lasts!* He thanked the Rector profusely and prepared himself to assist at the first service.

There was as usual only dear old Prudence at this early service and she too had been invited back to the Rectory for a little refreshment afterwards. All three braved the winds and were very keen to thaw out in the large Rectory kitchen. Following breakfast, they returned to St Jude's as it was the day of the important announcement regarding the eagerly-awaited horticultural show. Aubrey was convinced that the Rector was in such good humour for two main reasons. Firstly, Aubrey was to do the preaching that day and secondly, he was becoming not just a little excited about the horticultural show. In respect of the former, experience had taught him that Father Cyril was usually not so good-humoured after he had listened to Aubrey's 'pearls of wisdom,' and with regard to the latter, there was still a full six months until the show in September. He therefore felt sure that to keep a certain amount of civility for that length of time was likely to prove to be an impossibility! However, only time would tell.

The clergy party entered from the vestry and processed up the aisle. At this point Aubrey began to feel rather uncomfortable on three counts. Firstly, the big toe on his right foot was beginning to poke through an ever-widening hole in his sock and this was becoming rather obvious as he was wearing open-toed sandals. Secondly, a spider had begun to crawl up his leg inside his cassock and to his despair he had suddenly realised that, in his haste to get up so early that morning, he had failed to don any underpants! The thought of the spider rising into the 'no go' zone whilst he was preaching a sermon would indeed be his worst nightmare! The third area of major concern was the sermon itself. Aubrey was sure he had put the notes in his cassock pocket but all he could find there were two old shopping receipts. Uncontrollable fear began to seep into his body, and a shiver produced goose pimples all down his arms. In short, poor old Aubrey was yet again in a desperate state.

Lu Pipe, the organist, seemed in particularly good form that day as he had enjoyed some time in the company of some of his older pupils the previous night and he was quite convinced that some of the older girls found his eccentricity rather endearing. He was playing a new hymn and despite the restrictions of his current instrument, was making the organ sound a little more pleasing than usual. This was the hymn before the sermon and as he commenced the last verse with a very loud chord, Aubrey rose trembling into the pulpit. This was an open platform except for a wrought iron fascia which supported the book stand upon which most clergy would place their notes. Aubrey, however, simply placed the two receipts on the frame and in somewhat hesitant tones quoted his text.

"The gospel according to St Michael, beginning at the three pounds fifty, I mean the third verse," said Aubrey quickly as he tried desperately to come up with something whilst contemplating the Marks & Spencer's till receipt! "St Michael had three small bananas and a pot of yoghurt and he had to feed a crowd of five thousand people."

Aubrey hoped he could get away with just a short sentence of text and paused for inspiration. Whilst pausing, to his dismay, his toe had now become firmly lodged in a corner of the wrought ironwork and the more he wiggled it, the tighter the constriction seemed to become. Furthermore, he could feel the unmistakable sensation of the spider climbing his left thigh. Aubrey began to enter a state of complete and utter panic and the pitch of his voice began to rise accordingly!

"I wonder, I wonder, erm how many, that is, what number of people, perhaps a couple, perhaps three, maybe four......" droned Aubrey, desperately thinking on his feet, "could feed a crowd of five thousand people, that's not two thousand, or three thousand, or four thousand......"

"Oh do get on with it you blithering idiot!" said Cyril in a loud stage whisper.

"...but five thousand people with just three bananas and a pot of yoghurt?" frantically continued Aubrey. "I have in front of me a till receipt and on this till receipt is written 'three bananas and a pot of yogurt'."

At this point, the spider had climbed another few centimetres and Aubrey started to move up and down, as unobtrusively as he felt able with one toe stuck in a wrought iron pulpit, in order to jog the spider downwards! Cyril peered over his spectacles, quite incredulous at the sight of his curate bouncing up and down in the pulpit whilst debating the varying merits of three bananas and a pot of yoghurt! He had been convinced that Aubrey was unusual, yea even eccentric, but this performance was positively bizarre!

"In order to make three bananas and a pot of yoghurt go around five thousand people it is best to shake them up and down," squeaked Aubrey becoming more frantic by the second. "And then you give each person just a taste, the merest taste, only a taste, just a taste!"

As Aubrey spluttered out the last few phrases, his speech became quicker and quicker and the pitch of his voice higher and higher. The spider was showing no sign of being displaced and Aubrey could feel it straying into an increasingly personal area!

"Sometimes in life," said Aubrey very quickly and in a painfully high pitched voice, "you need to believe that things are possible and then you may be surprised at what can happen!"

At this point, the panic of the situation, coupled with the sweat on his foot, resulted in the imprisoned toe becoming dislodged from the confining ironwork. Aubrey seized the moment to escape and ended his somewhat confusing oration with a large and loud 'Amen'. He then scuttled off down the aisle to the relative privacy of the vestry and jettisoned the roving spider from its position! Finally relieved and totally exhausted, he fell back into the vestry chair and took five or six very deep breaths.

Meanwhile, back in the church, Cyril was making the long-awaited announcement regarding the horticultural show.

"This special show will be held at the Manor on Saturday the tenth of May," boomed Cyril proudly, "and I do hope all of you will come, and that you will encourage your friends to come and take a full part!"

With that, Lou struck up with the last hymn, and Cyril processed back to the vestry with a minimum of ceremony. After all, Aubrey had destroyed whatever dignity and atmosphere there had been in the church a long while ago!

"What in the name of Beelzebub was the matter with you this morning Aubrey?" probed Cyril angrily once back in the vestry. "I very nearly sent for the men in white coats – I thought you had totally flipped!"

"You wouldn't believe me if I had the energy to explain," apologised Aubrey. "Let's go and say good-bye to the faithful at the church door."

Aubrey and Cyril both made their way down the north aisle to the church door and began to bid farewell to the congregation.

"Very interesting sermon Aubrey," said the Colonel, "That'll get me thinking for the rest of the day! I thought the story involved bread and fishes," enquired Prudence, not famed for her intellect!

"Oh, it depends which version of the Bible you read," said Aubrey quickly and moved swiftly to greet Mrs Bloomfield-Upton.

Mrs Bloomfield-Upton just gazed in disbelief at Aubrey and passed quickly by, giving him her usual disdainful glare as she did so.

"I think we had better discuss your preaching technique in some detail but I cannot face that now," said Cyril in exasperation.

With that, he made his way back to the Rectory where a large schooner of medium sherry helped to raise his suicidal mood.

Aubrey returned somewhat sheepishly to his cottage too, thankfully managing to locate his underwear! He also thought a stiff drink might well be in order!

Chapter 6
Planting Seeds Should Be
Easier Than This

Eventually winter gave way to spring, and by April many of the villagers were longing for the greatly anticipated horticultural show. They had started to plant a wide variety of seeds in their gardens in the hope that their produce might walk off with some of the much-coveted prizes.

The Rectory garden was very large but Father Cyril normally avoided gardening. He preferred to employ old Ned from the Manor to spend some time at weekends, faithfully keeping things under control. There was a large expanse of lawn with well-established flower beds and shrubs on each side. The lawn gave way to a hundred foot kitchen garden which, thanks to Ned, kept Cyril plentifully supplied with vegetables for a large part of the year. Cyril was determined to attempt to grow a large prime marrow himself and was very keen to rival Mrs Bloomfield-Upton, whose marrows were indeed legendary!

It was a sunny morning in mid-April, and it happened to be Easter Monday. Cyril was particularly tired after the extra services during Holy Week and Easter. He struggled to put on his little-used Wellington boots and then trudged somewhat unsteadily across the lawn to the garden shed. Cyril's portly frame made any exercise a major event, so every so often he paused and admired a particular shrub or plant. Ned was blessed with green fingers and the garden was looking particularly colourful. The azaleas were a riot of purple, pink, orange and blue, and were beginning to take over from the daffodils which were now on the turn. A carpet of pansies on the right-hand side of the lawn gave way to primulas and fuchsias, and right at the end, before the kitchen garden, stood the most beautiful lilac. Cyril slowly opened the door to the shed and grabbed a fork and a rake. He closed the door and opened the old wooden gate to the kitchen garden. He then stopped for a moment and sat on the old tree stump by the fruit cage to ease his breathing and to plan how he was to execute the difficult manoeuvre of bending down to plant the seeds! First of course there was another difficulty, the preparation of the ground which he hoped to do with the minimum of effort!

Five minutes passed and Cyril had psyched himself up for the somewhat daunting task. Gradually, using the fork as a crutch, he eased his ample frame into the vertical and began to move down the path to the spot where he and Ned had agreed the marrows should be planted. Cyril put his hand in his trouser pocket and was reassured when he felt the precious seeds. Now he had to turn the soil a couple of times with the fork, pull out the few weeds, and then plant them. It seemed simple when Cyril thought it through, but to actually complete the task was to prove a different matter entirely! He drove the fork hard into the Norfolk clay and tried to turn the first sod. To Cyril's despair, the implement would not move and despite goading and some verbal abuse, was stuck fast. Cyril leant on the fork, first from one side and then on the other, but to no avail. If even his weight was not going to shift it, what could he do now? With one last almighty shove, Cyril cascaded head over heels into a gooseberry bush! The well-used ancient fork had snapped in two!

"Oh, for heaven's sake!" yelled Cyril, whose earlier good humour was now giving way to utter despair. "I'm sure Alan Titchmarsh doesn't have this sort of trouble? Why does it always happen to me?"

He rolled backwards and forwards and eventually managed to extricate himself from the gooseberry bush. However, he had little success in actually restoring his clerical frame to the vertical. He tried kneeling and then pushing himself up, but his considerable girth prevented this and his energy levels were flagging very rapidly. In complete frustration, he lay back on the ground to restore his energy and looked very much like a beached whale, stomach uppermost towards the sky! At this point, Aubrey arrived at the Rectory, and not being able to raise any response from the front door, walked round through the side gate into the garden where he suspected Cyril may have been taking his customary siesta! There in front of him were the lawns, and he noticed the gate to the kitchen garden was ajar. There was no sign of the Rector however.

"Cooee! Anyone at home?...Hello?" yelled Aubrey.

For once in his life, Cyril was delighted to hear the ridiculous high-pitched voice of his frustratingly inept curate, and eagerly yelled back.

"Over here Aubrey! I'm stuck over here, near the confounded gooseberry bushes!"

Aubrey peered through the gate of the kitchen garden but was unsure what a gooseberry bush looked like. He cast his eyes around and then noticed what appeared to be a large mole hill at the far end of the plot! He gazed in amazement and then shrieked as the mole hill moved! The rounded hillock was swaying from side to side and a groaning sound added sound to the spectacle!

"Are you anywhere near that mole hill?" enquired Aubrey walking closer to investigate.

"What the blazes are you prattling on about?" choked Cyril breathlessly. "I'm over here you baboon near the gooseberry bushes!"

Aubrey followed the sound which indeed seemed to be coming from the direction of the 'mole hill' and then as he approached, could clearly see that the concave form was in fact no less than his esteemed Rector lying stomach upwards on the ground!

"Well I must say that is a rather a strange place to go sunbathing but I suppose you do get a modicum of extra privacy down here Rector old chum!" teased Aubrey with disrespectful mockery! "You won't get much of a tan though with all the old skin covered up – won't win the Mr Forling Down 'hunk of the year' competition I wager!"

"I am not sunbathing you blithering idiot, and I have no intention of entering any degrading tanned body competitions," said Cyril exasperatedly. "I am trying to plant marrows Aubrey, but have managed to break my one and only fork and now I am stuck. I can't get up. Please will you assist me because it's becoming very uncomfortable down here and I'm pretty sure a worm has just entered my left trouser leg!"

Aubrey was completely at a loss to understand how anyone could end up in a supine position having broken a fork? Surely this could not happen if they were only trying to plant a few marrow seeds but nothing was ever that straightforward in Forling Down and this was obviously not the time to understand the succession of events which led to Cyril's misfortune.

Just at that moment, Ned appeared at the entrance to the kitchen garden and he noticed Aubrey talking to the plants!

"Hi, Aubrey? What ya sayen' to that thar gooseberry bush? Are ya lookin' for a baby under it?" quipped Ned. "Moi owld marm used to say that orl babies used ta come from gooseberry bushes! Oi believed 'er for a few years but then I read this book abort storks so I now know the old bush theory must be an old woiv's tale!"

"I'm not talking to the bushes!" began Aubrey, "and I have little interest in babies Ned," he continued, trying to pull intellectual rank. "The Rector's got himself into a little bit of a situation here and fallen over whilst, would you believe, trying to plant his marrow seeds?"

"Must be a moighty 'eavy marra seed, tha's orl oi can say," chided Ned in his broad Norfolk drawl. "What's the weather loik down there, Rector?"

"Cut out all the wise cracks and get me up you two!" commanded Cyril, who by this time was even less inclined to appreciate the ridiculous attempts at humour by both the extremes of humanity towering over him. "I am in no mood for inane remarks but am VERY keen to rise to the vertical before the uninvited worm inside my trousers gets too far up my thigh!" At this point both Aubrey and Ned convulsed into hoots of uncontrollable laughter but eventually tempered their hilarity and finally managed to ease the Rector into the vertical.

They helped the Rector back to the Rectory kitchen and kindly made him a large pot of hot tea.

"Shall oi plant yer marras for yer Rector or would yer loik to have another roll in the pasture tomorrow?" enquired Ned.

"I am determined to plant my own marrows, Ned, but I would appreciate the loan of a fork," replied Cyril feeling considerably better. "It might be a good idea though if I next attempt it at the weekend when you are here just in case of any repeat of day's mishaps!"

"I think that's a splendid idea if you ask me, Rector," said Aubrey as he finished his tea.

"I'm not asking you, Aubrey, but thanks for the affirmation anyway," said Cyril. "Now, I'm going to have to ask you chaps to leave because I promised the Colonel I'd phone him about one or two arrangements for the show and I'm already a good deal later than I agreed. Can you see yourselves out? Ned, I'll see you tomorrow morning and Aubrey, don't be late for Evensong because Mrs Bloomfield-Upton's bringing her niece from Scotland apparently. There is every chance that the congregation will be twice the size tonight!"

With that, the visitors duly made their exit and Cyril collapsed into his favourite chair by the fireside, ready to phone the Colonel.

Chapter 7

High Drama at St Jude's

Ever since the PCC meeting, Lu Pipe had been simmering with rage. He had been extremely offended by Cyril's dismissive and hurtful remarks regarding his musical prowess and he was absolutely determined to do something to firm up the support of his fellow councillors, thus quashing Father Cyril's seemingly blinkered view of the future of the music at St Jude's. It was a very cloudy and overcast Wednesday evening in late March and Lu had decided that the best way forward was to secretly spend some time on his own practising the organ. He could then acquire sufficient improvement in his keyboard skills to convince Cyril that both he and the organ had some sort of a future. St Jude's was a rather cold cheerless building at the best of times, even with the rather limited lighting illuminated, and there were all sorts of creaks and unexplained noises coming from the ancient pews, beams and dusty ecclesiastical furniture. Lu didn't particularly like being on his own in this forbidding atmosphere so decided that he would be more at ease if he locked himself in.

"That will give me peace of mind," he whispered to himself, "just in case anyone should unexpectedly enter while I'm playing."

He made his way up the south aisle towards the ailing instrument, mopped a layer of dust off the seat with his red-checked handkerchief, and proceeded to find a relatively easy hymn in his *Ancient and Modern* hymn book.

Lu then had a worrying thought. Although he had keys to the main door of the church, he did not have a key to the large padlock on the wrought iron gate at the north door. What would happen if someone came along, thinking that the building had been locked, and then locked the padlock while he was still inside? He came to the conclusion that it would be eminently sensible if wrote a note on the back of the previous week's pew sheet. He could then place it in a very prominent position in the porch so that anyone approaching the gate from the church path would clearly see it and react accordingly. In very large clear script, he duly wrote:

'Lou Pipe is locked in the church – please do not put the padlock on the main gate'.

He then scurried back down the aisle and unlocked the door again. He placed the note prominently in front of the outside gate for all to see and then returned to the organ, ensuring that the north door was firmly locked behind him.

"That's better," he sighed, "I feel much more at ease now."

Lu started to play 'Be still for the power of the Lord' because he knew this was a hymn pompous old Cyril would soon be requesting as it was one of his favourites. At first he rather falteringly picked out the notes of the melody line and then plucked up the courage to try to add the left hand! This as usual proved to be a disaster and the resultant cacophony offended even Lu's somewhat undiscerning ear!

Meanwhile, Aubrey had decided to cycle to the village shop in order to acquire a packet of jelly babies to sustain him through that evening's television viewing. Conscious of the fact that his bike was not equipped with even a basic form of lighting, he zoomed off at high speed singing 'Onward Christian Soldiers' at the top of his voice! This disturbed a large flock of rooks from the large yew tree in the churchyard as he sped past, and as he skidded on the gravel outside the shop, he misjudged the distance required to stop safely and ended up headfirst in the litter bin adjacent to the ice cream sign!

"Knickers!" he yelped. "That hurt. Confounded grit! Why can't someone sweep the blessed stuff up? Then cyclists like me wouldn't suffer an indignity every time they jolly well ride past!"

He dusted himself down and carefully extracted a discarded peach stone from his left ear!

Cynthia Gumbrel had been running the village shop for over thirty years. Prior to that, she had taught at the village school so she had witnessed most things in her long and varied life. However she couldn't quite understand what on earth was creating so much commotion outside. She gingerly opened the door, causing the bell to ring as she did so. There in front of her was an extremely embarrassed curate in an even more dishevelled condition than usual!

"What on earth is going on?" she exploded in her school marm stentorian tone! "This sort of stupid behaviour will not attract my customers! Would you kindly ride your bicycle with more care and attention in future Aubrey, and please do not reshape my litter bins!"

"Really sorry old thing," blustered Aubrey, somewhat shocked, slightly dazed and shaken by his experience. "Just slightly misjudged the jolly old braking time required! I'm in need of some jelly babies Cynth!"

Cynthia did not appreciate being called 'Cynth' and came from a generation which demanded respect. She had little patience with Aubrey at the best of times.

"Do not call me Cynth," she retorted crossly. "What you need is rather more than jelly babies. You need a complete brain transplant, preferably designed for humans! Didn't that expensive Eton education provide you with any manners at all?"

Suitably humiliated by the whole episode, Aubrey did not tarry longer than was necessary. He carefully mounted his bike for the return journey, hoping for a slightly more hassle-free journey than before. As he approached the church lych-gate, he happened to cast his eye towards the church, noticing as he did that the wrought iron gate was still open. Aubrey applied his brakes, more gently this time, and dismounted. He was still very sore following the debacle outside the shop, and he was still feeling very brow-beaten after Cynthia's withering castigation! Somewhat curious, Aubrey hobbled up the church path.

"Bunter's left the flipping gate open again," he muttered. "Better lock the jolly old thing I suppose!"

He started to unlock the padlock from its position on the gate, at which point his eyes alighted on the note placed by Lu earlier.

'I AM LOCKED IN THE CHURCH', he slowly read, squinting in the gloom to make out the unclear letters.

"Golly! Lu's in trouble!" he shrieked, bounding up the path as best he could in his tender state. Grabbing his bike, he scooted over to the Rectory to dispatch news of the apparent drama at the church. He leapt off his bike, letting it fall to the ground, and stumbled up to the Rectory door. Aubrey then began hammering earnestly, hoping to arouse Cyril's consciousness as quickly as he could.

"What the blazes!" gasped Cyril who was dozing contentedly after a nice cup of tea and a toasted crumpet. "Alright, alright, I'm coming! Don't destroy the door you moron!" he bellowed, immediately recognizing Aubrey's distinctive high-pitched tones. Cyril opened the Rectory door ready to confront his pathetic curate once again.

"Lu Pipe's locked in the church!" shrieked Aubrey with mounting panic and terror in his voice. "I think he may have been kidnapped or even worse," pleaded Aubrey urgently. "Somehow he had the presence of mind to shove a note under the door when his captors weren't looking. We must alert the police, perhaps even the army?"

"Calm down, calm down," wheezed Cyril, incredulous at all he was hearing. "I'll call the police – you go back to the church and direct them once they arrive."

Cyril duly dialled nine, nine, nine, imploring the control room to dispatch officers quickly to attend a potentially serious hostage situation. Meanwhile, Aubrey scuttled back to the church, forgetting all his previous aches and pains, as pints of adrenalin now raced through his veins. He stood terrified outside the church porch, not wishing to put himself in danger or alert Lu's possible captors. He then heard high pitched sounds coming from deep inside the building. Not realizing that Lu was still trying desperately to create some sort of recognizable hymn tune, he immediately assumed that he must be undergoing some sort of gruesome torture. Lu must surely be in terrible pain and agony now?

Within minutes, amidst sirens and flashing blue lights, six police response cars, two fire engines, an ambulance, a bomb disposal team, the county's trained armed response squad, and the police helicopter were all in position outside the church. In addition, a team of trained police negotiators with loud hailers began to attract the attention of all those inside the building. Search lights were erected and trained onto the outside of the building, and the booming sound of the chief negotiator started to pierce the usually still night air. A large crowd of villagers started gathering too, frightened by all they were witnessing in their usually very quiet hamlet.

"The church is surrounded. There is no escape. Give yourselves up. Do not do anything foolish," boomed the Inspector through the loud hailer.

Inside Lu immediately stopped his playing, as much as anything, blinded by the bright lights trained onto the building.

"What on earth is happening?" he spluttered to himself, shaking uncontrollably as the nightmare began to unfold in front of him. He stumbled down the south aisle, desperately fumbling in his pocket for an elusive church key. Once at the door, and in great trepidation, Lu turned the key very slowly in the lock, eased the door open, and gradually peered out into the glare and noise which confronted him.

"Don't do anything foolish!" blared out the loud haler. "Come out slowly and calmly with your hands on your head."

"Please don't shoot," stuttered Lu like a frightened child. "I'll do anything you say."

Lu slowly but surely put one foot in front of the other and made his way very slowly out into the porch, then into the cold night air. He was completely overawed by the mass of blue flashing lights, the din and downdraught of the police helicopter, and the continuing boom of instructions from the police inspector. Very quickly, a posse of armed officers ran forward, grabbed him roughly, and placed him handcuffed, and unceremoniously into the back of an awaiting police car. Another group then moved forward and into the church, searching every nook and cranny for evidence of hostage-takers or captors, but none of course were found!

It very soon became clear that the huge expense of the operation, the disruption to the tranquil life of the village, and the near heart attack suffered by Lu Pipe were all due to the somewhat hasty appraisal of the situation by the ever catastrophe-prone curate. Aubrey once again protested his innocence to the inspector and flatly refused to accept that he had wasted police time and resources. Cyril was less supportive of his case, indicating to the assembled officers that he was prone to stupidity and ineptitude, and that he had very little idea of what should and should not be done. In short, he was, explained Cyril, somewhat cerebrally challenged! Lu was not going to forget this day. He feared that every time he was to subsequently enter the church, he would suffer flashbacks and nightmares, and this, as he predicted, was certainly not going to bode well for his future mastery of the church organ! Cyril, more exasperated than ever following this ridiculous episode on a quiet weekday evening, made his way back to his desk to begin to pen a long detailed letter to the Bishop! It was entitled:

'Please remove my curate before I suffer an irretrievable nervous breakdown!'

Chapter 8

Suffering the Bishop's Ire

Bishop Hubert was a formidable character of the old school of clerics and he lived at Longley Hall, a very large rambling stately home about fifteen miles from Forling Down. Cyril was not in awe of many people, but he was very wary of erring on the wrong side of this particular bishop, something he had come very close to doing on more than one occasion! They had history and this dated back to their time together at theological college. Hubert found Cyril extremely tiresome, mainly because he was always far more interested in ceremony and ritual, than liturgy. He had little time for Cyril because of his laziness and pomposity, and it was the final straw when the two of them had been paired up to train together in neighbouring parishes in a fairly rough area of Southend in the seventies. This mixture of complete opposites was like mixing sodium and water! On numerous occasions, sparks flew and tempers raged. Cyril was actually quite frightened of him.

Bishop Hubert was a very overweight, imposing character and blessed with far more innate intellect than Cyril. The Rector loathed the fact that his bête noire had overtaken him in the promotion stakes too. Cyril had been appointed to the parish of Forling Down some years earlier by the previous Bishop of Norwich. It had been decided that he could do rather less damage in a relatively quiet rural parish, and now both Cyril and Hubert were less than overjoyed to discover that they were both working in the same diocese.

Now Cyril's desire to write about Aubrey had to be balanced against drawing too much attention to the various shortcomings of St Jude's Parish, not least the state of the finances and the consistently falling attendance at services!

Cyril poured himself a large glass of his favourite vintage port and desperately tried to formulate what was to prove a very difficult letter. Eight times he started writing and eight times he screwed up the sheet of paper in frustration.

Was he ever going to find the right words or was he going to have to accept what he feared, that his long sentence of tolerating his inept and irritating curate would have to continue? With a very deep sigh and a large gulp of port, Cyril attempted version number nine:

St Jude's Rectory
Forling Down
Norfolk

'Dear Bishop Hubert,

I send you greetings from the clergy and parishioners of St Jude's, Forling Down.

Whilst talking of clergy, you will recall that I agreed to accept Aubrey Crediton-Smythe as my curate some twelve months ago? He has faced a number of challenges over this period and it is my considered opinion that, because of his relative immaturity, he would benefit from a change of parish. This would serve to broaden his parish experience and, although he is clearly enjoying country life, I think a more urban parish would offer him new horizons and different opportunities. These in turn would prepare him for taking on his own parish in years to come, always assuming that you feel he would ever be ready for this?

I am very happy to visit Longley Hall to discuss this possibility should you feel this desirable and you should know that, as yet, I have not discussed this possibility with Aubrey.

With kind regards as always,
Yours in Christ,

Cyril
Rector of St Jude's, Forling Down

Still not sure if this missive was going to achieve its aim, Cyril carefully folded the letter, placed it in an envelope, and addressed it to the bishop. As the post box was very close to the Rectory, he found a stamp in his desk drawer and trudged the fifty yards to ensure it was safely on its way.

"Please God may I be freed of this impediment," pleaded Cyril to the Almighty as he placed the letter into the box.

*

The next day, Cyril's letter duly arrived at the Bishop's impressive residence. His housekeeper Doris knocked on his study door and placed it, together with the other post, on the Bishop's desk.

"Post late again," barked the Bishop, "Anyone would think we lived in Outer Mongolia not rural Norfolk! Thank you anyway Doris. That will be all."

Bishop Hubert, reluctantly moved from his armchair to his desk and began the chore of attending to the post which was never the favourite part of the day. Eventually, he came upon Cyril's letter, and he proceeded to slice it open with his brass letter knife. His blood pressure began to rise from the moment that he realized from whence it had come and as he read on, his cheeks became more ruddy and his patience gradually evaporated. Fuming, Bishop Hubert reached out for his telephone and proceeded to dial the number for the Rectory at St Jude's.

Back at the Rectory, Cyril was just finishing a late breakfast of boiled eggs and hot buttered toast. He was startled as his phone began to ring but Cyril was in good humour that morning. As a bit of fun, he often used to answer the phone by saying 'Bishop here!' when people from the parish phoned and usually this provided great amusement for all concerned. However today was not the best day to be perpetuating this charade.

"St Jude's Rectory, Bishop speaking," announced Cyril as he swallowed the last morsel of toast.

"Bishop?" said Bishop Hubert quizzically.

"Yes, Bishop speaking," continued Cyril, gleefully keeping up the usual merriment.

"Bishop Hubert here," was the stern reply as Hubert began to realise that one of his errant clergy was impersonating him.

"Oh God!" spluttered Cyril, at it gradually dawned on him that this was not the best day to be flippant.

"No, Bishop will do," retorted Hubert. "What on earth are you playing at? I assume I am talking to you Father Cyril?" he continued sternly.

"Ye...Yes," continued Cyril very nervously – not a characteristic usually associated with the Rector of St Jude's, but Bishop Hubert always had this effect on him.

"I have your disappointing letter in front of me, Rector, and yet again, the parish of Jude's seems to be causing me some annoyance. I assume there is a sub-text to this, something you are not telling me, and I resent this very much indeed. If you do not feel able to cope with training curates, you must be straightforward and say so. If this is not the case, you must show some backbone and get on with your parish and diocesan duties without 'namby-pamby' complaining. Do you understand where I'm coming from?"

"Of course Bishop," whispered Cyril, hardly able to speak through his fear and embarrassment. He quickly realized that pursuing this path was not going to bear fruit, so acquiescence was definitely the preferred way forward! "Please forget I ever wrote the letter Bishop, I will redouble my efforts to accommodate his eccentricities. We all have our rod to bear."

"It is a very small rod to bear in the scheme of things Rector, please refrain from contacting me again on this or any other related matter. Good day to you!" With that, Bishop Hubert slammed down his phone, ruing the day that he had anything to do with the parish of St Jude's!

Cyril was in complete and utter despair. He had misjudged his course of action totally and acted in far too much haste. If only he had waited a day or two, he might have come to a different conclusion, notwithstanding his frustration at having Aubrey in his parish. Now he still had him to cope with and in addition, he had an angry Bishop on his radar. Poor Father Cyril, fell to his knees and exhorted the Almighty to support him in this terrible hour of need.

Chapter 9
A Dastardly Deed

It was now early May and for a month at least, the dramas in Forling Down seemed to be fewer in number. Father Cyril was gradually coming to terms with having Father Aubrey as a curate and his mind was pleasantly preoccupied with the excitement of the approaching horticultural show. Not least on his mind was the prospect that he might even win some prizes!

The day before the Show, there was a hive of activity at The Manor. Marquees were being erected and temporary gardens and displays were being lovingly created. Thankfully the weather was set fair and everyone in the village was in good spirits. The Colonel had generously agreed to fund the hire of the marquees so Cyril was very optimistic that some well-needed funds might be raised to help prop up the very fragile church finances. There were cut flowers for sale; wrought iron artefacts from the village forge; fresh vegetables, home cooked pies and cakes; hot dog and ice cream tents; and of course the usual competitions. Cyril was particularly looking forward to the marrow growing competition as his offerings had put on quite a marked growing spurt over the previous two weeks, mainly thanks to Ned's loving watering and tending.

At about four o'clock, Cyril made his way slowly to the kitchen garden to cut his large marrows from their plants, carefully placing them on an old sack in his trusty wheelbarrow.

"Afternoon, Father," chirped Ned as he passed by the garden entrance. "Let me wheel 'em up to the Manor for you. Can't have any 'arm comin' to the prizewinnen' marras can we?"

"Most kind," said Cyril. "I'll see you up at The Manor after I've popped into the church for Evening Prayer."

With that, Cyril slowly crossed over the road to St Jude's, and Ned made his way up the lane to the Manor.

By five o'clock, Cyril had staggered up to the Show Ground and was delighted to see his super-sized marrows proudly and prominently on the display table.

"Tremendous," sighed Cyril, "If they don't win a prize, I'll eat my hat."

"Better get eating then your reverence," said a cheeky voice from behind him! It was unmistakably that of the ill-disciplined and habitually cheeky Rodney Hitcham. "My jolly old marrows are amazing this year and should clearly win the twenty pound prize!"

"Yours?" said Cyril imperiously. "Where are they? I don't see any marrows larger than mine you cheeky upstart."

"Oh, I'll be bringing them up later," stuttered Rodney, and with that, he flounced off through the marquee entrance.

Unbeknown to Cyril, Rodney was planning a dastardly bit of mischief. He was determined to win the prize money but had some relatively pathetic looking marrows by comparison. He had brought a syringe filled with weed killer and he planned to inject the poisonous substance into Cyril's marrows when his back was turned, thus ensuring that his would be the only decent ones to be judged the following morning.

Cyril slowly shuffled around the different displays, very encouraged by what he saw, and then, more than satisfied, left the big tent. Rodney grasped his opportunity, slipping in through the rear entrance. Hiding his syringe under a copy of his daily newspaper, he crept towards the marrow display table. Nervously, he glanced left and right, and when satisfied that the coast was clear, he surreptitiously injected both of Cyril's marrows with a phial full of the poison, smirking unkindly as he did so. He then skulked back through a gap in the tent wall, depositing the syringe in a bin by the entrance.

At the other end of the field, Aubrey had been asked to look after a pen full of various pets ahead of the traditional Pet Show. He nervously eyed up the empty enclosures which would soon be filled with an eclectic mix of livestock the following morning. He soon began to realise the enormity of the task ahead. This was surely not the wisest decision that the organisers had made, as it was common knowledge that Aubrey was extremely organizationally challenged and not the epitome of patience either! Promised for the Show were three guinea pigs, two ferrets, a gaggle of geese, two Persian cats (on loan from Mrs Bloomfield-Upton), a large Doberman, three alpacas and a large tank of valuable tropical fish! Aubrey's body was gradually consumed by impending doom, and he rapidly realized that the potential for disaster loomed large! The Colonel had arranged for various low fences to be erected, plus some sturdy tables, small cages and a power supply to service the fish tank. However, it was clear that having a Doberman adjacent to a gaggle of geese was going to be a recipe for a great deal of noise and possibly much worse!

As the light faded and dusk fell on Forling Down, Aubrey along with all those who had worked so hard during the day to prepare for the big event, began to stagger wearily back to their homes. Some eagerly looked forward to the big day, but Aubrey was less than excited at the role that he was destined to fulfil!

Back in the produce marquee and in the eerie gloom, Rodney's sabotage was beginning to take effect. Cyril's marrows were gradually turning from green to yellow, and were clearly in the early stages of wilting. The previously firm flesh was becoming a tender mush and they were certainly not now the fine specimens they were just a few hours earlier. How would the Rector react the following day and would Rodney's unkindness be discovered? Only time would tell. It was likely there would be anger as well as disappointment in equal measure. However, would justice prevail and would the perpetrator receive his just deserts?

Chapter 10
The Day of the Show

Cyril pulled back the curtains of his first floor bedroom at The Rectory, and the early morning sunlight poured in. Sadly after all the lovely weather of the previous two weeks, it was now very overcast and despite the early sun, there were black clouds looming on the horizon. The church bells chimed six and the cockerels were crowing in Forling Farm at the far end of the village. Despite this disappointing weather, Cyril was in pretty good spirits and was certainly looking forward to the much awaited and first ever Forling Down Horticultural Show.

"Rain before seven, clear by eleven," muttered Cyril hopefully as he staggered to the bathroom. "Please God may the weather perk up and may warm rays of your glorious sunlight shine down on our country enterprise!"

After completing his ablutions, Cyril treated himself to two soft boiled eggs, some buttered toast and a large cup of freshly ground coffee. He was confident that this was going to be one of his better days, despite the early morning drizzle, so he eagerly donned his clerical cloak, picked up his umbrella, and walked across the road to unlock St Jude's.

He then made his way slowly up the lane to The Manor, already beginning to bustle with eager exhibitors.

Other villagers were also starting to make the journey up the lane to the Show Ground as heavier rain began to fall. The earlier drizzle soon turned into a very heavy shower and this was threatening the success of their much-awaited special village event.

Aubrey had not had a good night and had slept rather fitfully. He was desperately worried about the pet show and realized that there was still enormous potential for disaster. He couldn't face much breakfast but forced down a rather over-ripe banana in the hope that this would sustain him for a few hours. Having poked his head out of the door and seen the impending deluge, he quickly donned his waterproof poncho and grabbed his bike.

Much to everyone's relief, the clouds moved off to the east and warm sunlight began to flood the showground. It was now nine o'clock and Colonel Wagstaff strode towards the microphone in the main marquee to proudly declare the Forling Down Show officially open. A few hardy villagers had braved the angry elements earlier and more were now eagerly filing up the lane. The loyal villagers began to part with their money as flowers, plants and refreshments were eagerly flying off the tables.

Life in the pet arena was not going so well as Aubrey had feared. He was nearing despair as the Doberman was barking furiously at the geese; the ferrets were straining at their cages to get near the guinea pigs; and the alpacas were clearly very frightened, and were frantically trying to escape their pens, shaking the table bearing the fish tank in the process. Seeing Aubrey flit from cage to cage and pen to pen was like an excerpt from a 'Carry On' film. Although this was quite distressing for some of the animals, it was providing some unplanned entertainment for the younger attendees in particular who were not averse to shouting mocking advice to the increasingly desperate curate!

Rodney Hitcham, never wishing to miss an opportunity to rib his old school pal, was making less than helpful remarks from the sidelines too, and was hugely enjoying witnessing Aubrey's despair!

"Why not sing them a lullaby old fruit!" yelled Rodney. "Might frighten them into submission!"

"Not in the slightest bit funny," puffed Aubrey who was unsuccessfully trying to put a lead on the over-excited Doberman. "Please tell the Colonel that I need help urgently – I fear a massacre if these beasts are not parted soon and I'm beginning to fear for my own life!"

"Sorry old boy," said Rodney, "must get myself a hotdog – hunger pangs are calling!"

With that Rodney flounced off towards the hot dog stall, and Aubrey was left to continue his fight with the Doberman, one he had clearly yet to win.

Life was considerably calmer in the main marquee, despite the weather, and Cyril strode over to the marrows on display. The sight that greeted him quickly wiped the grin off his ruddy face. His prize marrows which were looking so healthy and fulsome the previous day, were now more like yellowing, withered courgettes and certainly not likely to win any prizes. They looked particularly pathetic next to Rodney's rather splendid, yet smaller marrows and Cyril's blood was beginning to boil. There was no way this disaster could have happened naturally and the Eton tear-away Rodney Hitcham was the chief suspect in Cyril's eyes.

"What the bloody hell has been going on here?" boomed Cyril, incandescent with rage. "These marrows were perfectly healthy yesterday evening and there is no way that even an evening in a closed marquee would cause this degree of deterioration. Once I discover who is at the bottom of this, I cannot be held responsible for my actions. There is only one other person with a clear motive to destroy my prize marrows and that is that miserable reprobate and scoundrel, Rodney Hitcham. Where the bloody hell is that apology for a human being? Just wait till I get my hands on him!"

Rodney was hiding behind the preserves' stall looking just a tad sheepish. Had he gone a bit too far with this ploy? He had never seen the Rector so angry and there were now many villagers consoling him and assuring him of their support to get to the bottom of the incident. There rapidly seemed to be a posse forming, like something out of a spaghetti western, and Rodney Hitcham was clearly in the firing line. Rodney tried to find a way out of the marquee, trying to appear the embodiment of innocence, quickly formulating a plan to deny all knowledge of 'marrowgate'! After all, no one had any proof that it was him after all.

"There he is!" shouted Pricilla Grindthorpe in a high-pitched scream, pointing towards the jams and marmalades.

All heads turned and Rodney started to shiver with fear, his cheeks turning a bright red as blood rushed to his head. How on earth was he to extricate himself from this lynch mob, and how was he going to successfully deny any knowledge of the incident? After all, acting was certainly not one of his strongest attributes.

"Look what has been found in the litter bin adjacent to the marquee?" boomed the Colonel striding from the tent entrance towards the marrow display. In his hand was of course the offending syringe used by the miserable Rodney Hitcham the previous evening.

"Th...That's nothing to do with me" stuttered Rodney, now surrounded by a baying crowd of angry, noisy villagers, all accusing him of despicable sabotage.

"I've never seen it in my life, honestly I haven't," pleaded Rodney.

"Well you won't mind Constable Jones taking some fingerprints then will you?" demanded the Colonel. "He is on his way and should be here very shortly. In the meantime, Rodney Hitcham, you will not be going anywhere – I am making a citizen's arrest."

Rodney knew the game was up and he realized that his prints would be all over that syringe. He had not been clever enough to wear gloves and consequently it was only a matter of time before everyone in the village would know that he had sabotaged the Rector's prize-winning marrows.

"OK," said Rodney, hoping the ground would swallow him up. "It was me. All I wanted to do was to win the confounded twenty quid – I didn't want all this hassle and I certainly wouldn't want to really upset you, Rector. It was just supposed to be a bit of fun, but as usual, I've taken things a bit too far."

At this moment, the Forling Down police panda car drew up beside the tent and Constable Gareth Jones made his way into the tent. Everything was explained to him and Rodney was roundly admonished for his thoughtless act.

"I could charge you with criminal damage" said the Constable, "but instead I shall recommend that you volunteer to work unpaid in the churchyard for two months as a small way of repaying the Rector for your thoughtless act. Are you prepared to accept this course of action, or would you rather be arrested and taken to court?"

Reluctantly, Rodney agreed to the Constable's terms and sheepishly left the showground feeling very much like the naughty schoolboy who had been found out. He knew that his already flimsy status in the village was now completely in tatters and the thought of having to do physical work in the churchyard was the worst possible punishment!

Back in the marquee, Mrs Bloomfield-Upton and the Colonel were at the marrow display about to announce the results of the competition.

"Due to the disqualification of one of the competitors," announced Mrs Bloomfield-Upton in her usual stentorian tone, "the winner of this year's marrow-growing competition is our much-loved Rector, Father Cyril! They may not be the finest specimens but in the circumstances, I think the Rector is the deserving recipient of the trophy and the twenty pound prize."

Cyril had experienced the full range of emotions over the previous two hours. He had known real anger and despair but was now bathing in a great deal of love from all his parishioners and, of course, absolute delight that he had won the much-coveted prize. The trophy would adorn his mantelpiece in the Rectory and the twenty pound cheque would ensure the purchase of another bottle of his favourite vintage port!

Chapter 11

The PCC Meets Again

Three weeks had now passed since the horticultural show and the PCC was gathered once again in the Upper Room at the 'Newt and Ferret' pub. Father Cyril was still in relatively good humour following his triumph at the Horticultural Show. However, a sense of foreboding was consuming him as he cast his eyes around the table at the usual eccentric array of humanity before him. These meetings rarely went smoothly and Cyril nearly always experienced great difficulty in controlling the competing factions which displayed varying degrees of competence.

Aubrey and Rodney were smirking at some risqué magazine under the table, and Pricilla Grindthorpe was shuffling a great pile of papers covered in figures and analysis which Cyril feared might precipitate a lengthy discussion. Lu Pipe was still feeling anxious about his future as church organist but was determined to try to tough it out if he possibly could.

Cyril thumped the table to gain the attention of all present. With his usual superior air, he said a short prayer and proceeded to start the proceedings without further delay.

"Are there any apologies for absence?" he enquired.

None were forthcoming so he proceeded to peer over his spectacles at Pricilla, the church treasurer, enquiring about the current financial position of the church? He was desperately hoping that affairs had improved since the dire situation apparent at the previous meeting.

"Well," began Pricilla in her usual condescending tone, "the books do show a mild improvement in the current account following the receipts from the Horticultural Show which raised just over eight hundred pounds after expenses. However, this will in no way cover the parish liabilities over the next twelve months and I fear we are about to default on our diocesan quota yet again."

At this point she stared straight at the Rector, clearly wishing to provoke a response. Cyril hated financial matters, not least because he did not understand them, and he always dreaded any discussion which involved him making decisions about money, or in the case of St Jude's, the lack of it.

Eventually, after what seemed ages, Cyril took a deep intake of breath and adjusted his spectacles. "It is abundantly clear to me," he began somewhat tentatively, "that we need to either attract further funds or make some further economies."

This prompted another lengthy silence. Cyril knew that his comment was naive in the extreme and almost embarrassing in its simplicity. Pricilla was checking down her list of figures once again and Cyril was not at all clear what more to suggest.

Edwin Jones, the village butcher let out a very loud snore! This prompted Mrs Bloomfield-Upton to sit very upright, resting her ample chest on the table.

"I will say it again," she began imperiously. "We clearly need to save money and the obvious starting point is to dismiss our desperately inefficient and incompetent organist. Mr Pipe has been here for more years than I care to remember and I'm still hoping against hope, that we shall be able to enjoy a service sometime soon, devoid of wrong notes and any semblance of dynamic variation! Furthermore, the pedal board is so dusty, it clearly hasn't seen a foot for many years!"

Aubrey and Rodney broke into uncontrollable laughter as Lu Pipe, the much-maligned organist, looked ready to explode, his cheeks becoming redder by the minute.

"This is just not fair," blurted out Lu who had been fearing a further verbal onslaught at the meeting. "Who around this table feels they could do any better? I have worked for many years to acquire my Grade three piano certificate and with continuing practice, who knows, I might even manage Grade 4!"

Mrs Bloomfield-Upton cut through the conversation with another fearsome verbal exocet! "Most church organists can boast a musical degree and some letters after their names sir. The only letters which you can display, Mr Pipe, are BF or US, and your meagre retainer is an absolute waste of our almost non-existent and rapidly diminishing income!"

Lu was an interesting mixture. In many ways he was an introvert who shunned the limelight, and it was true that his keyboard skills did not compare with those of most church organists, even those in more rural parishes. However, there was a stubborn, determined streak to his character which rose to the surface when he felt threatened and today was indeed such a day. He felt bullied and he considered that he had been dealt a very unfair hand. Why should he be used as a scapegoat to solve the church's finances? Was he not doing his best with a very substandard instrument and a virtually non-existent choir? Lu suddenly felt emboldened and sitting bolt upright, addressed the assembled company.

"When I joined the congregation of St Jude's some ten years ago, I was welcomed warmly. I thought I was amongst friends who would appreciate my efforts, however humble. Over the years, I have felt increasingly bullied and demeaned and this is just not what I consider to be a Christian approach."

He felt a sweat forming on his brow so he reached into his trouser pocket to locate a handkerchief. He took two deep breaths and mopped his brow, clutching his hanky for further use. Lu was about to make a suggestion that would stun the Rector and the PCC. There was a crescendo of murmurings around the table but Lu was determined not to cave in and loudly continued with his desperate plea.

"I am prepared to work incredibly hard to give an organ recital! I will expect no payment and no fee. I also propose that the choir is reformed and augmented, so that I can include some beautiful choral music as well. I would suggest a ticket price of £10 per person, to include a glass of wine in the interval, and all proceeds can go towards the restoration of the church finances. This is not much to ask – I am determined to prove to you that I am more than an object of ridicule in the eyes of many in this village. I am a human being with feelings, and I want for once, to be taken seriously."

At this point, Lu's voice rose in pitch to the point where it sounded as if he might burst into tears.

Father Aubrey had been hugely moved by Lu's desperate 'crie de coeur' and he immediately offered his support.

"Come on dear chap," he began consolingly. "You are a much-valued member of this community and of course we should support this very generous offer."

Cyril was not convinced but unusually was just a little sympathetic to the organist's plight. Mrs Bloomfield-Upton was less understanding and was not taken in by Lu's dramatic, yea even melodramatic outburst.

"How on earth do you propose to deliver an organ recital when you find it incredibly difficult to accompany a simple hymn without fluffing eighty percent of the notes?" she exclaimed imperiously. "As for the idea of re-forming the choir again, well I'm more likely to be selected for the Great Britain gymnastics squad than for that to be a success!"

Colonel Wagstaff, often the voice of maturity and calm, cleared his throat. "I think it is only right and proper that we give Mr Pipe an opportunity to prove himself and, whatever has happened in the past, one has to agree that this is a very generous offer. Do you agree with me, Rector?"

The Rector had been completely taken aback by Lu's outburst. He was certainly not one of his supporters but he did feel somewhat compelled to give this crazy idea at least a chance.

"If Mr Pipe can make a success of this," began Cyril, "then we shall all be very grateful." He shuffled in his chair and proceeded to continue. "I suggest the rectal takes place on St Jude's Feast Day – October 28th. We can have a Patronal festival Eucharist in the morning with a special recital in the evening. All those in favour?"

The assembled company felt compelled to agree to the Rector's suggestion and Lu Pipe was clearly exhausted, but delighted with the outcome. All he had to do now was to somehow increase his keyboard skills to such an extent that paying customers might actually feel that their money was being well spent.

The extended discussion about the finances and Lu's unexpected intervention had meant that the meeting had grossly overrun. Downstairs the bell was being rung for last orders so Cyril declared that the meeting was closed.

This had indeed been a very unusual evening, even by Forling Down standards so Cyril was even more than usual, salivating at the thought of a small glass of port accompanied by some biscuits and Stilton, seated in his favourite armchair in the Rectory. After a few minutes, happily this all came to pass, and Cyril once again was able to relax in the security of the Rectory after yet another challenging day.

Chapter 12

Planning the Concert

As dawn broke the next day, Lu Pipe began to absorb the enormity of the task ahead and gradually came to terms with what he had promised to do. He must have been mad. He had admitted to himself that his keyboard skills were extremely limited for a church organist and as for the choir, well there wasn't one to speak of, and he had no evidence to suggest that there was an appetite to reform one any time soon. He paced about the house wracking his brains for inspiration and some sort of spiritual guidance, but none seemed forthcoming. Point one, how was he to improve his technical ability to achieve even a modest chance of performing for a paying audience? Point two, how would he attract singers to a choir when he knew that he possessed, as one previous chorister had jibed some months previously, "about as much charisma as a lettuce leaf!" Desperation was firmly setting in and a huge sense of panic started seeping through his veins. A warm sweat began forming on his brow and real despair was beginning to pervade his entire being. He certainly couldn't face any breakfast and the cup of tea he had made half an hour previously was now very lukewarm and uninviting.

Suddenly there was a loud knock at the front of his humble terraced cottage. Reluctantly, he dragged himself up and slowly opened the door. There in front of him, beaming from ear to ear in his usual inane way was Father Aubrey!

"What ho old thing!" chirped the lanky curate, "thought I'd come to see how you were old chum! I thought the jolly old committee was a bit harsh last night and that you deserved better mate! How about a nice cup of tea and a good old chinwag eh?"

"That's really kind of you Aubrey," sighed Lou, immensely relieved that at least someone seemed to be on his side. "I'm really panicking about this wretched concert – was I completely mad to propose such a thing? I was so desperate to rescue my fading self-esteem that I spoke without really thinking the whole thing through. Please help me Aubrey – I'm feeling almost suicidal."

Despite his eccentric outward disposition, Father Aubrey was actually a very kind, sympathetic and empathetic human being, and he could understand completely how poor Lu was suffering. He'd been there himself after all, on many occasions.

"Let's have that cup of tea old boy and we can talk the whole thing through," said Aubrey reassuringly. "Everyone has a supply of God-given talent and you are no exception. We can make this thing a real success chum, I know we can. It just requires some really careful planning – we'll make this jolly old concert the talking point of the village for many years to come, and for all the right reasons!"

"I'm afraid it will be the talking point for all the wrong reasons," sighed Lu! "You can't make a silk purse out of a sow's ear, as they say!"

"You are not remotely like a sow's ear!" quipped Aubrey reassuringly. "You and I are going to sock it to 'em my friend – I have contacts…and a few jolly old favours to call in, and now is the time to reap some of those rewards!"

Lu set about making the tea and the two sat at the kitchen table ready for their 'council of war'! Aubrey himself was often the butt of jokes and teasing, so he felt that he also had something to prove. This concert could be just the right vehicle to silence all the soothsayers of doom in the village as well as those who were always quick to make hurtful jibes at them both.

"Have you got a pen and a bit of paper old chap?" enquired Aubrey, relishing the fact that he was in control for once! "Let's start making a few notes and plan this jolly old thing carefully."

Lu willingly provided some paper and a pencil and carefully placed two cups of tea on the table. Aubrey proceeded to make a list of all his old Etonian chums who had gone on to enviable musical success in a variety of genres, while Lu ferreted around to locate his biscuit barrel! Within a few minutes, both had succeeded. Lu had located the barrel under some cushions in his sitting room, and Aubrey had dug deep into his memory to create an impressive list of old school friends, some of whom were now household names!

Despite Aubrey's somewhat eccentric and hair-brained persona, he could actually be quite a good organiser if he put his mind to it. He started to map out a possible template for the concert programme, hoping to include a wide variety of musical styles to suit a variety of tastes.

"Let's start by thinking big," explained the animated curate. "We can always slim things down a bit later if things don't work out. We need some fab musicians to accompany items and then we need some jolly good soloists. My rather frightening house captain at Eton was the orchestral conductor Gustav Less – I think he's currently with the Munich Radio Orchestra and he certainly owes me a massive favour. He knows that I am the only person in the whole universe who is aware that he pinched dear old Matron's pink lace bra, then hauling it up the Big House flag pole just as the Queen was arriving to open the new Arts Centre! There was a huge stink about the whole jolly affair and to this day, Gustav has not been implicated! He knows that I spotted the prank from my dorm window and he begged me never to split on him in case he got the jolly old "heave ho" from the school! I'll definitely send him an email – just imagine having Herr Less and the Munich Radio Orchestra playing in little old St Jude's Church? That would most certainly put us on the map! More tea I think Lu – I've got my juices going really well now!"

Lu was aghast at the tone and calibre of the concert's potential and hardly dared to contemplate an evening on such a scale. Could it really come to pass? If it did, his 'street cred' would indeed rocket and never again would people dare to humiliate him or his abilities. Aubrey continued to scribble his thoughts and ideas and Lu duly re-boiled the kettle in order to replenish the pot.

"Right, I think we're sorted, old boy," exclaimed Aubrey! "We'll start with the jolly old National Anthem played by the orchestra and you on the organ of course! You can manage a few big chords OK old chum can't you? Then we'll have a set by the 1970s crooner Andy Grinter – he's often on TV panel shows these days but can still pump out a few power ballads when he wants to! He's the father of another one of my school chums, Wayne Grinter. Then we can have the church choir singing a short anthem, either accompanied by the orchestra or you on the jolly old organ, or perhaps both?"

Lu immediately chipped in bleating that there was no church choir and nobody seemed interested in coming back to sing any time soon.

"Lu, my dear old matey, who in their right mind would not want the chance to perform in a concert with the likes of Gustav Less and Andy Grinter? The jolly old parishioners will be queuing up to be in your choir, we might even manage to get the flipping TV companies to cover it for the local media – Forling Down is going to be VERY big news!"

"I just don't know what to say Aubrey," sighed Lu. "You are better than all my anti-depressant pills put together – I can't thank you enough!"

"Don't thank me too soon old boy – haven't got the acceptances yet, but I'm pretty damn optimistic! Now let's continue while the old brain is still functioning. After that bit, we'll get the orchestra to play again and then, how about a spot with Plectrum Eight, the pop group riding high in the jolly old charts at the moment led by Andy Grinter's son Wayne who, as I explained, also went to the jolly old school! By the way, I'm pretty sure Andy Grinter was at Eton with Sir John Downing who is now our Prime Minister of course – I wonder if we could persuade him to put in an appearance? Can you imagine the headline in The Sun – "Sir

John Downing hits the high notes in Norfolk village with Herr Less!" I suggest we finish the evening with everyone joining in together with a rousing medley of songs from the shows. Then we'll drag you up on stage to conduct Land of Hope and Glory at the end! Forling Down will absolutely love you and we should raise a fantastic amount of dosh for the jolly old parish in the process."

So the grand plan was set. Father Aubrey promised to contact the Eton alumni, the television companies and a staging company he knew; and Lu Pipe, only two hours earlier at his wits end and in deep depression, was now mildly euphoric, yea even heady about the possibilities of the success of Aubrey's plan. Could these amazing ideas really come to fruition? Only time would tell, but Lu was now more excited than he'd been for many years.

Aubrey thanked Lou profusely for the tea and the two comrades exchanged a very big man hug at the door. Aubrey then leapt once again onto his trusty bicycle en route to make these ambitious plans a reality.

Chapter 13
Progress Is Made

It was now two weeks since Lu and Aubrey had met. As promised, Aubrey had made contact with his suggested artists and to his enormous delight Gustav Less had at least agreed to discuss the possibility. This was not by any means a "Yes" but it was definitely a move in the right direction. Apparently the Munich Radio Orchestra was performing at the Royal Festival Hall in London on 27th October so the orchestra were at least in the country on 28th October and in theory, the date was free. As yet there was no word from Andy Grinter's agent or Plectrum Eight but Aubrey remained optimistic that his plans might still come to fruition.

The following day, Gustav sent a message to explain that he was coming to England the following week so Aubrey arranged to meet him in the foyer bar at the Royal Festival Hall to reminisce and to see what might or might not be possible.

When Aubrey had contacted his prospective artists, he had explained what the line-up might be, in the hope that this might tempt each into being part of such a high profile event. Incredibly it seemed to be working because later that day, Andy Grinter's agent phoned to enquire a bit more about what was involved and how it might work. Andy was apparently taking time off from concert tours in the autumn as he wanted to write some new material for a future album. Once again therefore, in theory at least, he should be available. Aubrey was really encouraged by these initial responses and was very optimistic that if Andy Grinter agreed to come on board, his son Wayne and Plectrum Eight would more than likely follow?

Just as he was getting deeper into impresario mode, Aubrey was unexpectedly startled by some loud knocking on his front door.

"What in heaven's name......!" yelped Aubrey, "OK, OK, I'm coming."

Leaping up in his usual somewhat eccentric manner, Aubrey lunged for the front door, and on opening it, discovered a very angry-looking Rector – red in the face and puffing to gain his breath.

"Where the blazes have you been Aubrey?" chided Fr Cyril imperiously, still fighting for breath. "Had you forgotten about the additional Thursday Mass at 10.00 a.m. this morning and furthermore, had you forgotten that YOU were supposed to be giving the homily? Not only did I have to prepare the altar, your job, preside over the service and clear up afterwards, also your job, but I also had to concoct a short sermon which was not on today's 'to do' list!"

Cyril leant on the door frame gasping for even more breath after this explosive outburst. Aubrey began to fear that he might have to start CPR if the Rector carried on in this excitable manner, and edged slightly closer, just in case the Rector took a turn for the worse!

"Oh my goodness!" pleaded Aubrey, "I am so, so sorry Rector – I was busy trying to help Lu Pipe organise his concert and I completely forgot the time, and I guess the day too. Please accept abject and heartfelt apologies? It will never happen again."

"I will accept nothing of the sort you apology for a cleric," blurted Cyril. "You were appointed to this parish as an assistant curate NOT as a show business consultant! I suggest you decide whether you wish to "feed the flock" or "hunt with the hounds" and when you've decided, come and explain your decision to me. Until that time, you will put your liturgical duties ahead of any other temptations – do you understand?"

Cyril took another huge intake of breath and glared over his spectacles at poor Aubrey who had now moved from elation at the prospect of his successful concert plans to the depths of despair and embarrassment following the Rector's very challenging outburst.

"Of course I understand my dear Rector," apologised Aubrey as meekly as he knew how. "You can rely on me to support you at all times in the future. I shall visit the church immediately and prostrate myself in front of the altar to seek forgiveness from the Almighty!"

"I am not your 'dear'," chided the Rector, "and there is nothing to be gained from imitating the posture of Thomas à Becket before the altar. I will see you at 5:30 p.m. for Evensong this evening and in the meantime, you can prepare the sermon for Sunday as penance for your lack of appearance today." With that, Cyril eased his frame through one hundred and eighty degrees and departed very slowly back to the Rectory, feeling rather better for getting those feelings about Aubrey off his chest yet again.

Aubrey gave a huge sigh, closed his front door, and collapsed into his armchair. How could his emotions have gone from such a high to such a low in just a few seconds? It all seemed so unfair. All he was trying to do was to help a mate who was in dire distress, and now he was once again being bullied by his superior? He sighed again thinking that perhaps 'bullied' was a bit strong, but he did feel very fragile and vulnerable at being at the receiving end of the Rector's caustic tongue.

Just as he was in the deepest depths of despair, deeper than he had experienced for some time, Aubrey heard a ping from his PC – a message had just come through. He dragged himself from his armchair and flopped onto his computer chair. There in front of him was a message from none other than Sir John Downing, his old school friend from the Bullingdon Club at Eton. He hadn't contacted him yet so why was he messaging him? He tentatively opened the email and squinted at the screen aghast that someone so famous should be sending him a message. It read as follows:

My dear Aubrey,

You are probably as surprised to be reading this as I am to be writing it! I have been informed by that old cad Andy Grinter that you are putting together a charity concert and that a number of old chums are likely to be taking part? Quite by chance, I am planning to do some election canvassing around that time in Norfolk to support our candidate up there, so making an appearance at this event would arguably enhance the chances of attracting some much-needed votes. Therefore old Bullingdon mate, if you can find a modest role for me in this jolly old evening, I should be delighted to take part? Perhaps I could do a spot of compereing or read a monologue – just don't ask me to sing!

Yours ever,
John

Aubrey could not believe what he was reading. John Downing, yes THE Sir John Downing, the Prime Minister of the United Kingdom, had just sent him an email, AND he wanted to come to Forling Down! Was he dreaming all this? No he wasn't, and it was all actually happening. He rapidly sent a reply to Sir John, eagerly agreeing to his proposal. This had restored Aubrey's faith in humanity and once again, he was in a good place. As he pressed 'Send', he fell back in his chair, offering thanks to God yet again for His grace and strength.

Onwards and upwards, thought Aubrey. *If I can make a success of this concert, not only will Lu and the parish be happy – I might even get a 'thank you' and some appreciation from the Rector!*

Chapter 14
Another PCC Meeting!

Since the fateful day when Aubrey had forgotten to attend the Thursday mass, much had happened to move the success of the concert closer to a reality. Aubrey had met with his rather intimidating old House Captain Gustav, who now seemed perfectly normal and reasonable – a far cry from those adolescent days at Eton where he was quite the opposite! They had reminisced for hours over a few beers at a hostelry in London, and to Aubrey's sheer delight and amazement, Gustav had agreed to bring the Munich Radio Orchestra to Forling Down, their small country village in Norfolk, in a bid to support the parish towards achieving solvency. It transpired that Gustav's great grandfather had lived in a neighbouring parish so he had an emotional connection with the county. He was also keen, amazingly, to support his rather eccentric fellow pupil and to wipe the slate clean as far as the 'lace bra' incident at school was concerned!

Andy Grinter, now aware that the Munich Radio Orchestra was to be involved, eagerly jumped on board and offered his services. He had been encouraged by Aubrey's promise to try to attract the interest of the local TV company, Anglia Television. Andy saw this as a great way to promote his latest recordings so there would be something in it for him too.

As predicted, once Andy had signed up, his son Wayne and Plectrum Eight felt obliged and encouraged to take part too for similar reasons, so the future of the concert seemed even more assured and far outweighed their original ambitions to use local talent.

Coincidentally an extra-ordinary PCC meeting had been convened by the Rector for later that week. He was blissfully unaware of Aubrey's amazing progress, so was preparing himself up to have another go at his much-maligned curate and organist Lu Pipe as he felt the proposed concert was hugely over ambitious and feared that it might result in the village becoming an object of national ridicule. Cyril felt that he was surrounded by imbeciles and each successive day seemed to illustrate yet another example of the ineptitude of so many of the country folk of Forling Down!

Aubrey and Lou on the other hand were in a very buoyant mood, absolutely bursting to share their exciting news! Rarely had either of them felt this degree of confidence before a PCC meeting and they just could not wait to impress and amaze their fellow parochial church councillors!

****

The day of the meeting arrived, a Friday evening, and once again the group convened in the upper room at the Newt and Ferret pub opposite the church. The usual suspects were present – Mrs Bloomfield-Upton sporting a very large blue hat; Colonel Wagstaff, smart as always in a tan checked sports jacket; Edwin Jones, the butcher still wearing his apron; and the somewhat intimidating church treasurer, Pricilla Grindthorpe, who like Cyril was working herself up mentally for a dismissal of the Lu Pipe concert idea as sheer fantasy and a lost cause! In contrast, a relaxed Fr Aubrey and Lou sat together at the far end of the table ready to release their exocets of glad tidings!

The church clock struck eight and Cyril thumped the table with his fist to instil peace and order.

"Good evening everyone," he began. "I think tonight more than ever we need the guidance and support of the Holy Spirit, so let us pray."

Cyril uttered a short prayer for strength and understanding and then called the meeting to order with a further thump of the table. Edwin had been dozing as was his habit, and this last thump startled him so much that his head shot up and the top set of his false teeth shot across the table landing on Mrs Bloomfield-Upton's ample chest, then drifting oh so slowly down her blouse!

"Oh Gawd!" she bleated imperiously. "What on earth are your teeth doing on my breasts?" she screamed. "Have you no control, have you no propriety, have you no consideration for the feelings of others?"

Edwin's cheeks became redder by the second and, as he tried to blurt out a few words of embarrassed apology, the pitch of his voice rose higher and higher.

"I'm so very, very sorry," he stammered, "would you like me to come over to retrieve them?"

"I do not want a butcher near my breasts thank you very much!" she retorted disdainfully, "I shall locate a clean tissue from my handbag and I shall extract your dentures myself. This is just beyond embarrassing and is becoming an absolute nightmare. Do you not use some sort of denture adhesive? This sort of behaviour is totally unacceptable and I demand an immediate apology!"

"I am REALLY sorry, Mrs Upton," began Edwin stuttering.

"**Bloomfield-Upton** Mr Jones, **Bloomfield-Upton**!" she blasted across the table. "How long have you lived in this village? How long have you known me? Do you not think it is about time you showed a modicum of respect for your elders and dare I say, betters?"

At this point Fr. Cyril tried desperately to refocus the meeting on the agenda and thumped his fist on the table for a third time.

"I'm quite sure Edwin did not mean to jettison his teeth in your direction on purpose Mrs Bloomfield-Upton," he began. "Once you have extracted the aforementioned molars, please pass them over the table back to their rightful owner, and perhaps the matter can be set aside. I am sure Mr Jones is more than apologetic and might even pass you a string of complementary sausages!"

Mrs Bloomfield-Upton tutted and grunted. Plunging her right hand down her top to locate Edwin's teeth, she then passed them unceremoniously across the table with an evil stare that would have sent shivers through even the toughest of humanity. Edwin meekly received them and thought better of returning them to his mouth immediately. "Better give them a good rinsing first I think," he muttered under his breath.

Cyril, having re-established some sort of authority at long last, explained that there was just one item on the agenda of that extraordinary meeting, the proposed concert scheduled for St Jude's Day.

Pricilla shuffled her papers of figures noisily, successfully attracting the attention she craved, and reminded the assembled company that the church finances continued to be in a dire state. She explained that only that morning, she had received a letter from the bank informing her that if a credit balance was not restored to the church account by Advent Sunday, the start of the new church year, the account would be closed and heavy penalties would be imposed. She ended by stating that her considered opinion was that the proposed concert idea was ridiculous and not at all likely to raise anything like what was required to stabilise the church's finances.

Now appraised and reminded of the current financial position, Cyril stared over the top of his spectacles in the direction of Aubrey and Lou who seemed to be unusually alert and relaxed, considering the dire warnings and forebodings uttered by others around the table.

Aubrey felt the need to stand up to address his fellow councillors. He drew himself up to his full height, cleared his throat and proceeded to explain the incredible progress that had been made since they had last met. As he recounted the huge array of talent promised for the event, he observed with huge delight, that the jaws of the others present had dropped open, and they were clearly dumbfounded by Aubrey's apparent effectiveness as an impresario!

"So my friends," he concluded, "all we need to do now is to establish a role for Lu in this exciting concert and I will do my best to ensure that the event is publicised far and wide. This is really going to put jolly old Forling Down on the map and I think Lu's street cred should also rocket as he performs with such a splendid array of talent. I hope this will end all the unkindness and teasing that has hitherto been all too prevalent in this parish. Lu deserves our complete and unfettered support, not our continual jolly old sniping!"

"Mr Jones's teeth need support," retorted Mrs Bloomfield-Upton, "but I have to give credit where credit is due, Fr Aubrey. We have often ridiculed you for your eccentricities and your privileged past, but tonight you have shown us your rather caring and supportive side, which I never thought I would publicly acknowledge or witness."

"Agreed," said the Colonel. "This is just amazing news and you both have my full support."

"Well I must say, I am flabbergasted," interjected Pricilla. "This does indeed present the distinct possibility that some serious money could be raised if we can pull this off. I congratulate you Aubrey on a considerable coup. Well done, Sir."

Aubrey flopped back in his chair exhausted but elated at the response. Now he and Lu would have to work really hard to ensure that the event really did go ahead, but he was much encouraged by the uncharacteristically warm responses from those present at the meeting.

"Well," said Fr Cyril, preparing to say what he never thought he would. "I think we should congratulate our parish curate on a considerable achievement. I never thought I would be publicly applauding Fr Aubrey after the gaffs of the recent past, but I feel duty bound, as Mrs Bloomfield-Upton has stated, 'to give credit where credit is due'. It is now your duty to ensure that these plans come to fruition. Now I think we should stand and say 'The Grace' together."

The traditional conclusion to PCC meetings was duly completed and the villagers made their way down the stairs to the main bar below.

"I feel a celebratory drink is called for," declared Colonel Wagstaff. "Place your orders at the bar and they can all go on my tab!"

"That's awfully civil of you, old boy," chirped Aubrey, enjoying his newly acquired popularity, "thank you Colonel!"

And so the night ended in a celebratory mood. The councillors relaxed in the 'Newt and Ferret', buzzing with real excitement as they discussed the unbelievable prospect of so many famous people coming to their small village!

Chapter 15
Lu's Dilemmas

Over the next few days, Lu tried to process the enormity of what Aubrey was proposing and how he could possibly match the incredible array of talent from the wealth of professional musicianship promised for the concert. How could he compete? How was he to gather together a choir which would not end up being the laughing stock? He was also waking each night in a cold sweat. He kept reliving the potential nightmare of performing on an organ with his comparatively modest keyboard skills in front of some of the country's top musicians. In desperation, he reached for his phone and called Fr Aubrey, the one person in the village who he felt he could trust. There was no reply. Aubrey must be out! Lu shuffled across his sitting room and collapsed into his armchair. He must come up with some sort of plan. He felt his stomach beginning to cramp, partly due to the fact that he wasn't eating properly, but in great part due to his utter panic and foreboding at his participation in such a prestigious concert. He couldn't sit still for more than a few minutes and proceeded to pace nervously backwards and forwards from his sitting room to his kitchen. He must try Aubrey again. He wiped the accumulating sweat from his palms and tried dialling. The phone rang and rang but Aubrey was still not answering, but then, just as he was about to replace the receiver, he heard the unmistakable sound of his eccentric friend on the end of the line.

"Curates pad!" chirped Aubrey, full of the joys of Spring. "Father Aubrey at your service!"

Lu cleared his throat and began to mumble some indistinguishable words of utter panic and desperation.

"I can't do it. I can't do it," he kept repeating, his voice becoming higher in tone as he repeated the phrase. He then started coughing and Aubrey became quite concerned.

"Who is this?" quizzed Aubrey, still not sure who was on the other end of the line.

"It's me, it's me!" shrieked Lou. "Lu Pipe, Lu Pipe. I'm desperate, I'm becoming suicidal, I'm feeling really ill! I can't do it, I can't do it. I REALLY can't do it!"

"Can't do what?" urgently enquired Aubrey, using all his powers of empathy to calm the panicked voice at the other end of the line. "You seem to be in a bit of a state old boy, just sit down, take some deep breaths and I'll pop round."

Lu hung up without saying another word. He was now feeling quite faint as well as having griping stomach pains and he now also had a thumping headache. He flopped back into his chair once again, just a little cheered at the prospect of the curate coming to comfort him. He reached into his pocket, once again taking out a handkerchief to mop his dripping brow. There was then a loud knock at the door.

"Ah, that must be Aubrey," sighed Lu, lifting his pathetic frame from his chair and stumbling towards the front door. He flung it open and beckoned Aubrey inside.

"Cripes old boy, what in the name of Beelzebub is the matter – you look as if you've seen a ghost? Put on the kettle and let's have another jolly old chat about it all."

Lu duly shuffled out into the kitchen clutching his painful stomach which felt as if it was being squeezed in a large vice. His head was still pounding and Aubrey could clearly see that he had managed to get himself into a very worrying condition. The two friends sat down, sipped tea and gradually Aubrey set about allaying Lu's fears.

After much discussion and reassurance, Aubrey explained that Lu's participation could be very limited – just enough to ensure that he was hailed as a star, but not enough to expose his shortcomings. During the National Anthem, Lu's organ (Aubrey always roared with laughter every time he said this!) would be centre stage with the orchestra fanned around him, but Lu's involvement would be to just play a few chords, doubled by the brass and strings so almost inaudible. This meant that there was no worry there. Regarding the choir item, Aubrey suggested that perhaps he might ask Herr Less to conduct, as a gesture of respect and friendship, thus relieving Lu of this ordeal too? They would together try to gather singers who could be persuaded to be involved – a task which should not prove to be too daunting, given how prestigious this event was now becoming.

As if a miracle had just taken place, Lu felt the tension in his stomach evaporating and the throbbing in his head turned to a warm sense of eager expectation rather than the previous fear and foreboding.

"Come round to my pad this evening old chap and we'll dot the 'i's and cross the 't's. This will go down as the most hip hop and happening event in the jolly old history of

Forling Down, perhaps even in the history of Norfolk! We can share a particularly fine bottle of claret together – I've been waiting for an excuse to pop open that jolly old bottle which has been gathering rather a lot of dust for some time!"

****

Later that evening, as arranged, Lou made his way down the main village street to the Curate's house where Aubrey was eagerly awaiting his arrival. He had uncorked the ten year old vintage claret given to him by Mrs Bloomfield-Upton the day he arrived in the parish. Two freshly polished glasses stood next to the bottle ready to be filled, and an array of crisps and other nibbles completed the mouth-watering array on the coffee table in his front room.

Lu nervously lifted the brass knocker on Aubrey's front door but almost leapt out of his skin as the door swung open, whipping the knocker out of his hand before it had had time to sound! Aubrey chirped an almost child-like greeting as he excitedly ushered the somewhat reticent organist into a comfortable armchair. Aubrey was in his element and hugely excited by the potential of the extraordinary concert being planned for such a small, sleepy country village.

He poured the rich red claret into the gleaming glasses and the ideas flowed increasingly easily as the level in the bottle reduced! Aubrey had already outlined a programme, keeping Lu's involvement to a minimum, yet still making him feel valued and included, but reducing the earlier fears and stresses that were causing the reluctant organist so much agony and dismay.

After well over two hours of excited deliberation (and the consumption of a second bottle of less expensive red wine!), the two agreed to arrange a more formal meeting at the Newt and Ferret at the end of the month, rather hoping to attract some of the performers as well as the village hierarchy. Aubrey thought that putting on a formal dinner in the upper room usually used for PCC meetings would create the right atmosphere, and unusually Father Cyril agreed, realising that his hitherto troublesome and irritating curate had at last seemed to have found his vocation.

Chapter 16

Dinner at the Newt and Ferret

It was a Friday at the end of July and the dinner invitees began to gather in the upper room as planned. Unusually, every member of the PCC was intending to be present and Aubrey had, after some considerable effort, also managed to secure the attendance of Wayne Grinter (of Plectrum eight fame), the son of seventies star Andy Grinter, now in the twilight of his career but still a very popular panellist on various game shows and late night chat shows.

Unusually, Cyril was actually looking forward to this event. It had the twofold advantage of providing him with a free meal (generously underwritten by Colonel Wagstaff on this occasion), and the prospect of solving the parish's dire financial forebodings, at least in the short term.

Just as most of the locals had found a place and ordered a drink, there was a deep throaty roar of a powerful engine outside, none other than that of the vintage Jenson Healey driven by Wayne Grinter.

"What the blazes is that extraordinary noise?" enquired Cyril, almost choking on his pre-dinner pint of Norfolk ale.

"Sounds as if a spaceship 'as just landed if yer ask me!" drawled Ned in his broad Norfolk accent.

"I suspect this is our jolly old VIP," chirped Aubrey, with a mixture of nervousness and anticipation, having not seen Wayne since his school days at Eton.

He scurried down the pub stairs almost demolishing a tray of drinks being carried up by Clare, the youngest of the pub barmaids.

"Careful old boy," she yelped, somehow managing to rescue all the liquid orders skilfully but not thanks to the excitable curate. "Sorry, old girl," whispered Aubrey, "bit of a hurry tonight I'm afraid!"

Outside the pub, Wayne recognised Aubrey immediately! He was still the eccentric, lanky and unpredictable buffoon he had known and teased unmercifully at Eton but that was all to be forgotten now.

"Thanks so much for gracing our humble village with your esteemed presence," said Aubrey, giving Wayne a big man-hug as he stood in front of his impressive wheels! "That's a pretty fab old chariot Grinty, must have cost a bomb?"

"Hi you old fool!" beamed Wayne, "still as mad as a hatter I see! Yep, it did set me back a few quid but you can't take it with you, can you? Where's the party old boy, 'lead on Macduff!'"

"Thanks so much for coming old chap," continued Aubrey, "we're all upstairs waiting for you, do follow me and I'll introduce you to everyone!"

Aubrey led the star through the saloon bar as all the regulars paused their drinking and looked aghast and incredulous as the TV personality and much-loved recording artist strolled through their humble pub. Were they imagining things or was this really happening. As the two started up the stairs, there was an excited buzz in the bar below as everyone tried to take in what they had just seen!

Aubrey and Wayne entered the Upper Room and once again a hush fell on the assembled company.

"Hello everyone," said the somewhat star-struck curate! "This is my old school-mate Wayne Grinter who of course needs no jolly old intros from me!"

"Hi, chaps," replied Wayne, "pleased to be with you tonight and pleased to be able to support your very exciting venture. I can't believe Aubrey has managed to pull this thing off – my memory of him was not even to be able to organise his laundry at school, let alone delve into the realms of being a successful impresario!"

Aubrey blushed, embarrassed at these gentle chidings, but realised that his old school chum had meant it all in good humour. He showed Wayne his seat and introductions were given around the table by Colonel Wagstaff who was assuming the role of Chairman for the evening.

Just at that point, two of the pub girls appeared in the doorway ready to take orders for dinner.

"Excellent timing," announced the Colonel. Let's order starters and mains and we can see how we feel about desserts in due course. "Girls, can we have a few bottles of vino on the table too – I think a bit of fine grape will help the ideas to flow!"

The girls duly took orders and discussions started regarding the proposed programme, the building of a large stage in the church, the laying on of additional power and the provision of loos – nothing was to be left to chance.

Just as the starters arrived, there was an incident involving Ned Gaskin (retired farm worker and part-time verger) and Priscilla Grindthorpe, the church treasurer. Ned had carelessly dropped his spoon on the floor as he attempted to unravel his serviette – an item of tableware not usually provided in his cottage! Ned eased his hair back slightly and proceeded to fumble on the floor area underneath, leaning into the lap of Ms Grindthorpe as he did so.

"Excuse me, Mr Gaskin! What on earth do you think you are doing?" she screeched imperiously. "Why is your head approaching my skirt area and why in heaven's name is your hand flitting backwards and forwards adjacent to my ankle?" Her volume and pitch increased as Ned pursued his quest to retrieve his item of cutlery! "I absolutely insist that you exit my personal space Gaskin – get away from me NOW!"

"Awful soorry Ms Grindthorpe – oive mislaid moi spoon see, and oi need ut if oim gonna be able to eat moi soap! Aah – think oi may av found it – yes, 'ear it be, sarry bowt that moi dear – all is well now!"

"I AM NOT YOUR DEAR!" shrieked Priscilla, "don't you ever venture near me again in that very provocative manner, or in any manner come to that. I knew it was a mistake sitting next to you!"

"Thaat's a bit offending Ms Grindthorpe – oi was only pickin' up a metal spoon – no need to declare world war three ole gal!"

At this point the Colonel had heard quite enough and invited the Rector to say Grace. Cyril gladly responded, embarrassed by his parishioner in front of an important guest!

'Spoongate' aside, the evening meal and meeting was very constructive and all present were becoming increasingly excited at the prospect of this very ambitious concert. Publicity was going to be a key factor and Andy had promised considerable help in this regard, he having many very useful contacts and opportunities.

Three hours, three courses and five bottles of wine later, the party broke up, agreeing to meet again at the Manor House on August 28th, just two months ahead of the concert date. It was all getting very real now.

Chapter 17

Forling Down to Be on Television?

Father Cyril was feeling very replete and not a little inebriate after the excesses of the dinner at The Newt & Ferret. He had not stinted himself with regard to portion size or choice of dishes and he had definitely lost count of the glasses of Chateau Neuf du Pape that he had consumed! Luckily it was only a short distance from the village pub to the Rectory so he shuffled gently from side to side, keeping a respectful few feet from the hedge, as he slowly edged his way to his front gate. It creaked open allowing Cyril to achieve the final few yards to his front door, thankfully without incident!

He never made it to his bed that night but rather flopped into his favourite chair, falling into a deep sleep as soon as his head touched the back against a perfectly placed cushion.

At eight o'clock the following morning, he was rudely awakened by the Rectory phone. After the previous night's indulgences, this seemed painfully loud!

"What the blazes!" muttered Cyril as he quickly realised where he was and what was shattering his peace. Thankfully the phone was by his chair so he slowly stretched across, fumbling for the receiver. As he grasped the handset, the sound mercifully ceased, allowing Cyril to refocus and gather his wits about him.

"St Jude's Rectory," he growled, clearing his throat as he spoke. "Father Cyril speaking."

"Good morning, Rector," came the reply. "My name is Benedict Cussack and I am calling from the forward planning section of Anglia Television in Norwich. I gather you are mounting a rather splendid concert in Forling Down on St Jude's Day this year with a most impressive star line up including the music legend, Andy Grinter? I wonder if I might come down to discuss the possibility of us featuring this event on the Anglia News and…possibly even recording excerpts from the evening for transmission later this year as part of a documentary on Andy?"

Cyril fumbled for his spectacles and tried to make sense of this very unexpected phone call. His head was still very woozy from the previous night's indulgences, and processing this unexpected proposal was not coming easily! There was quite a long silence as Cyril tried to bring himself into the present reality.

"Are you still there Rector?" interjected Benedict, "sorry if I've caught you at an inconvenient time?"

"Yes…I'm still here!" yawned the Rector, "I had a late meeting last night and awoke a little after my usual time this morning. This is all rather unexpected and I don't usually welcome a lot of outside interference in church matters."

"Let me stop you right there if I respectfully may," interrupted Benedict. "You may be interested to learn that a considerable fee would be paid to the church for allowing this coverage and I know most churches would welcome some extra revenue?"

"Ah, I see," said Cyril, gaining more interest by the second! "I'm glad, you mentioned that small fact which could well sway the opinion and response of the Parochial Church Council. When would be convenient to visit us?"

Looking at his diary, "I could meet you next Friday at about 10:00 a.m.?" said Benedict.

"That would probably work," choked Cyril who was still suffering with an early morning frog in his throat. "I would suggest we meet in St Judes Church, and I'll try to muster as many members of the PCC as I can so that we can expedite matters as quickly as possible."

"Excellent," replied Benedict, "I look forward to meeting you and many of your council members on Friday next at ten in the morning – Goodbye!"

"Goodbye," said Cyril, hardly allowing himself to believe all this sudden good fortune. Could it really be that this nugget of an idea of a parish concert could really be morphing into a major television event with all the inherent good publicity and money that it would bring to the parish? "Thank you Lord," gasped Cyril. "You certainly do work in mysterious ways!"

****

Early the next morning, Fr. Cyril tried to phone Mrs Bloomfield-Upton to try to arrange an extraordinary meeting of the PCC. He was very frustrated to learn from her housekeeper that she was at the hairdresser's having yet another purple rinse! She did arrive home about an hour later though, and duly phoned Cyril to try to discover what new barmy idea he wanted to impose on the parish this time!

"Mrs Bloomfield-Upton," said Cyril with renewed confidence and command. "I have some extremely exciting and potentially transformative news regarding our proposed fund-raising concert and it is imperative that I talk to the PCC without delay. Please would you be kind enough to gather the troops together this evening in the usual room in the Newt and Ferret? Time is of the essence – we must not delay or a once in a lifetime opportunity may be missed!"

"I cannot imagine what is so important, Rector," replied Mrs Bloomfield-Upton in her usual patronising and superior tone. "It is my bridge night tonight and I normally have an unwritten rule that nothing is to interfere with Bridge Night."

"I really must insist that we meet tonight," interrupted Cyril. "If we meet without you, so be it, but we must gather this evening."

"Oh very well," sighed Mrs Bloomfield-Upton in a very exasperated huffy manner. "I am beyond curious to discover what on earth could be exercising your mind so importantly that you need to call a crisis meeting so urgently."

"Believe me, it is no crisis," retorted Cyril. "Quite the reverse. I think you will soon realise why I need to talk to you all tonight. I will see you at eight o'clock and expect everyone else to be present at that time – goodbye!"

Mrs Bloomfield-Upton was consumed by a mixture of emotions. These ranged from utter frustration that a PCC meeting of all things was about to interrupt her bridge evening, to incredulous curiosity at what on earth could be so important?

Overcoming all these conflicting emotions, the PCC was duly called together, and later that evening gathered curiously in the village pub to discover the eagerly awaited news.

Chapter 18
Cyril Shares the News

Fr Cyril thumped his chubby fist on the wooden table in the pub's upper room and a sudden hush descended. Unusually, all the PCC were in attendance. They were more than just a little curious as to what could possibly be so important that a meeting of the church council had to be called at such short notice and so soon after the last one.

"My friends," began Cyril in an unusually warm and measured tone. "You will all know that our proposed fund-raising concert is scheduled for St Jude's Day, October 28th, this year. We are a small yet important country parish in rural Norfolk but despite our modest means have amazingly managed to secure the services of recording sensation Andy Grinter; his son Wayne and his group Plectrum 8; internationally renowned conductor Gustav Less and the Munich Radio Orchestra and would you believe it, Sir John Downing, has offered to compère the event! It pains me to say this, but I must express considerable gratitude to my generally somewhat eccentric curate, whose school day connections have made all this possible."

"Why, thank you, Rector, for those jolly nice remarks," interjected Father Aubrey! "Always happy to be at your service!"

"I wish you weren't at most services!" muttered Cyril under his breath!

He then, peered over his round spectacles and tried to continue, frustrated by the uninvited interruption!

"So why on earth, you may all say, do we need to gather this evening after a very long and detailed discussion at the last meeting?"

"Indeed," said Lu Pipe the organist, yet again fearing that this was going to be yet another occasion when his future at the church was to be compromised. "This was all agreed last time and I was going to be fully involved?"

"Nobody is saying that you aren't going to be involved Mr Pipe, although that is a very attractive suggestion," muttered Cyril aside to Colonel Wagstaff. "I implore you to stop interrupting, and to allow me to finish."

Cyril shuffled his papers and regained the place he had reached in his notes...

"Well my friends, yesterday afternoon I had a phone call from a gentleman called Benedict Cussack, who is from the forward planning department at Anglia Television based in Norwich. Word has made its way to his office that we have, quite amazingly, managed to attract an extraordinary line-up of star musicians for this humble concert and now he is suggesting televising the event so that highlights could be transmitted both on the news, and on a special documentary that they are planning. My initial reaction was to graciously decline their kind offer but then came the offer of a considerable broadcasting fee which would be payable, not only to the artists performing but also to the venue, i.e. St Jude's Church in Forling Down! My sincere hope is that you will all accept this quite extraordinary God-given opportunity to swell our funds and suspend any of your usual inclinations to fend off media intrusion into our village life?"

The gathered company was left open-mouthed at this unforeseen development. There were various intakes of breath and it was Priscilla Grindthorpe, the Church Treasurer who finally broke the silence.

"Rector, this is indeed a most unexpected offer and one that I feel we should all accept with open arms. Not only will it bring in much needed funds for the church accounts – but it will also raise the status and profile of Forling Down and possibly, dare I say it, even bring us national recognition!"

Colonel Wagstaff, normally very suspicious of media intrusion, also spoke warmly in favour, as did Prudence Pots who was getting giddily excited, rather like a teenage girl, at the prospect of TV cameras and Pop stars in her village.

"Oid better think abowt payin' ma jolly old TV licence I spose," drawled Ned Gaskin, St Jude's rather simple part time verger! "Oi 'avent watched anything much really since the fifties! Is Eamonn Andrews still doin' 'This is Your Life?'"

"Oh for heaven's sake," interrupted Cyril. "I haven't got time for all this nonsense! If you carry on with all this ridiculous nonsense Ned, YOUR life will be in danger! Now," Cyril, continued hurriedly, "We must have a vote on this – all those in favour of Anglia Television covering the event, please raise your hands." Unsurprisingly, following the earlier comments, there was unanimous support, and every hand was duly raised.

"I think it is time for a celebratory drink," declared Colonel Wagstaff. "Go to the bar downstairs everyone and order a drink on my tab once again. Aubrey, that does not run to bottles of Moet Chandon however! Please curb your usual temptation to take advantage of my kindness, and order a more modest beverage on this occasion!"

"Well really Colonel – that was quite uncalled for!" said Aubrey with a glint in his eye. "I shall be my normal abstemious self!" The Colonel gave him a very old-fashioned look but slowly saw the funny side and gradually broke into a modest grin.

The assembled company, in an extremely and unusually united mood, made their way down the narrow pub staircase to the public bar and thoroughly enjoyed celebrating Forling Down's new and exciting good fortune!

Father Cyril, after more than a few glasses (he had actually lost count!) of a rather splendid vintage port, staggered with a broad smile on his face, back to the Rectory. Today had been a very good day and he thanked God for all His many blessings!

Chapter 19

Benedict Cussack Comes to Town

Following the extraordinary PCC meeting, there was a great buzz in the village. Everyone was talking about the concert and it was certainly the only item of conversation in the village shop.

Lu Pipe, the church organist, was doing his best to hone, or perhaps acquire his keyboard skills. It was an open secret that these were sadly lacking at the best of times and merging Lu's skills, or lack thereof, with those of the Munich Radio Orchestra was going to be a very big ask! There was going to have to be some very clever planning if both were to be performing together.

A big meeting had been arranged for the following Saturday at ten o'clock in the morning. It was to be held at St Jude's which, like many Norfolk churches, was built in the late medieval period during the thriving wool trade. It was thankfully pretty big by parish church standards, and it would need to be, given the ambitious plans being formulated. Those due to attend this very important meeting were Fr. Cyril, Fr Aubrey, Lu Pipe, Colonel Wagstaff, Benedict Cussack from Anglia TV, and Chas Grundy, Andy Grinter's agent. Chas also had contacts with the Radio

Orchestra so he was clearly going to be a key player in all these preparations.

Cyril had not slept much the previous night. His nocturnal trials and tribulations were a mixture of excitement and modest anxiety about the concert, and a nagging big toe on his right foot – the result of a flare-up of his intermittent gout!

Prudence Pots and Ned Gaskin had opened the church very early, just before seven o'clock, in order to prepare the coffee and refreshments. Prudence had made some homemade shortbread biscuits which, if one was being charitable, were a tad hard baked! Ned had brought some fresh milk from the farm and had extracted cups and saucers from the cupboard at the back of the clergy vestry. Prudence and Ned did not really get on. They were both somewhat cerebrally challenged! Prudence in particular was your stereotypical simple country girl and Ned had worked on the land all his life. He was a hardworking farm labourer, having worked at the Manor for over forty years. Neither could list organisation as one of their exceptional skills but, having said that, they were both willing souls, albeit not necessarily singing from the same hymn sheet! They argued about where the refreshment table should be situated but, in the end, Ned won the argument and erected it in the bell tower at the back of the church.

"We can't 'ave it at the front," he drawled, "as all 'em important chaps are goin' ta be talkin' up there 'bout the concert ain't they?"

"What if the bell ringers decide to come and do some practice while we're serving?" countered Prudence in her high, slightly whining voice. "I really don't want to get into trouble with the tower captain?"

"Nao chance a' that," said Ned. "When was tha last toim ya saw or 'eard them pullin' bells at noin a'clock in tha mornin'? Use ya loaf Prud – the bell tower is tha only sensible place – end of!"

Prudence shuffled out in a huff and Ned put two tables out in the tower. One of the spare altar cloths was laid over them and the crockery was put out ready.

It was now a quarter to eight in the morning and Fr. Cyril arrived to say Morning Prayer in the Lady Chapel at the top of the south aisle. He grunted greetings to Ned and Prudence. Fr. Cyril was not a morning person and at any rate, would have found it very hard going to make any meaningful small talk to those two! Cyril gathered together the necessary books and sat himself in the stall in the chapel.

"Where the blazes is my inept curate?" he muttered under his breath. "I do hope I'm not going to be here talking to myself yet again – Lord please give me the patience of Job and the wisdom of Solomon! I must have been very bad in a previous life to deserve my present assistant cleric!"

Just then the heavy oak door creaked open and Father Aubrey raced up the aisle in his habitual breathless state.

"Rector, you will never believe what happened........"

"No I wouldn't and I'm not interested Aubrey, you blithering idiot – please sit down, gather yourself together, and prepare to meet your Lord!"

"Of course, Rector," apologised Aubrey, feeling yet again like a naughty schoolboy in front of his headmaster.

Morning Prayer then passed without further incident with each of the priests playing their part in the daily ritual.

Unusually, Ned and Prudence had also joined them in the chapel so the Rector was able to record an attendance of four – double the usual number!

As the church clock chimed at a quarter to ten, some cars could be heard arriving on the gravel area outside the church. The Colonel was first, closely followed by the willowy form of Lu Pipe, the church's artistically challenged organist and Director of Music!

"Morning Pipe!" barked the Colonel in his plumy cultured tone. "Got some real musicians coming to the church this morning old chap. Best to keep a low profile I think – don't want to upset anybody!"

"Well that's a bit below the belt Colonel and quite uncalled-for I say. I have every right to be here AND to speak if I feel I want to. I may not be wealthy but I have feelings!"

"Please yourself!" retorted the Colonel. "Just don't want you to make a fool of yourself and more importantly don't want you to scupper any of our very exciting plans. You do know you have a history of being somewhat indiscrete?"

This knockabout conversation was thankfully brought to a halt by the arrival of Benedict Cussack and Chas Grundy who had both shared a taxi from Norwich Station. The assembled company were warmly greeted by the Colonel and Fr Cyril and then were politely ushered to the back of the church. Coffee was being served by Prudence, who was quite awe-struck at the arrival of Benedict and Andy in particular!

"Would you like one of my lovely homemade shortbread biscuits your honour?" said Pru in a high-pitched, rather childlike voice to Benedict.

"Very kind," replied the television executive. "I'm not a judge so no need for the extravagant titles! Perhaps you would like one Chas?"

Chas Grundy was a bit of a fitness fanatic and therefore rarely indulged in snacks. "I think I'll pass dear if you don't mind, but they do look delicious! Pass them round the rest – we don't want emaciation setting in do we?"

"Pass them over here, Pru, old thing!" called out Aubrey, "Never turn down an offer of a jolly old biscuit!"

"Can I encourage you all to take a seat," invited the Rector, somewhat exasperated yet again by his irrepressible curate! "We have so much to discuss and I know you are all very busy people."

Everyone duly found a convenient chair and Fr. Cyril explained the aim of the concert. There was the need to raise much-needed funds for the church due to falling numbers in the pews and an ageing congregation. He also explained the desire to replace the church organ, also very much ageing, and the projected expense of this. Cyril then dug deep in order to be as diplomatic and charitable as he could be, without being dishonest.

"Our organist is Mr Ludevic Pipe," said Cyril, identifying Lu at the table.

"Known locally as Lu Pipe!" convulsed Aubrey who then broke into hysterical and uncontrollable laughter!

Cyril cleared his throat and tried to make light of his frustration at Aubrey's interjection. "A little local in joke," said the Rector trying to bring things back to the point. "Now as I was saying, these are the main reasons for holding the concert and it is beyond wonderful that professional musicians have volunteered to support us, and the icing on the cake is the potential involvement of Anglia Television – we are indeed enormously grateful."

"Extraordinarily grateful," interjected the Colonel. "And what is as important as all of that – our parish community will be united in a common cause and our village should be a beacon of hope throughout Norfolk, showing what can be achieved if everyone works together."

"Jolly exciting too!" chirped Aubrey. "Will be great to see some of my school dorm chums again what ho? Haven't seen some of them since we all organised an apple pie bed for our headmaster! He was beyond livid but never discovered who it was! Between you and me, it was Sir John's idea! Who would have thought? Just look at where he is today!"

"That sounds like a great TV story Fr. Aubrey," said Benedict, always on the lookout for a sensational angle. "I think we'll have to do an interview with you at some point!"

"Oh yippee!" blurted the excitable curate. "Lots more where that came from!"

Fr. Cyril, using all his powers of control and determination, brought the discussion back to reality and very useful plans were made for the big day. Benedict explained the technical requirements of running an outside broadcast. A number of large trucks would need to be accommodated in the church car park. There would need to be lighting trucks, sound trucks, a large Director's truck full of screens, and some generator trucks as it was quite clear that St Jude's ageing 240 volt circuit would be grossly overloaded by the demands of all the broadcast equipment.

"I think we can probably survive without a catering truck, but we shall require portable toilets if the church can provide these facilities Rector?" enquired Benedict?

"You can also use the facilities at the Manor," added the Colonel – "it's only two hundred yards up the road."

"Excellent!" said Benedict. "What would be the needs of the musicians Chas? I guess the orchestra has about eighty players and their instruments would need to be stored securely? Then there are the needs of Andy, Wayne and Plectrum Eight. On reflection, I think we will need some hospitality vehicles too in the car park to accommodate the stars attending?"

Colonel Wagstaff interjected again. "I will make the Manor available to you for the orchestra's needs. You can use the great hall as a base and this will be locked securely during the performance. There are of course plenty of toilet facilities too so no problem there."

"Will Lu be having a jolly old hospitality truck?" joked Aubrey, yet again bubbling up another hysterical laugh! "He is our star organist after all – he can play various things as long as they are in the key of G Major!"

"Well really!" sighed Lu, most embarrassed at being humiliated in front of such distinguished company. "You really are a lousy cad Aubrey and not nice at all. Call yourself a priest of the church? I thought clergy were supposed to be thoughtful and charitable to their flock?"

Fr Cyril, not unusually, was becoming increasingly frustrated and annoyed yet again, at Aubrey's schoolboy humour and temptation to engage in juvenile spats with anyone who he deemed to be in a lower class to him.

"Forgive these village idiots" exclaimed Cyril, yet again trying to bring matters to a sane level and trying to make light of his embarrassing curate's intervention. "Forgive this country banter Benedict and Chas. All meant in a good heart I can assure you!"

"That's all fine I think," said Benedict, slightly amused by the eccentricities of Forling Down. "I'll be in touch and we can firm up any minor details by phone or post I'm sure."

"Sure I really can't tempt you to a biscuit," Said Pru.

"Best avoided oi reckon" said Ned. "We down't want ta put these koind people orf naow do we?" drawled Ned who had been dozing throughout most of the discussion.

Cyril, yet again, was getting more than a little embarrassed. "Thank you all so much for taking the trouble to come down to St Jude's and even more thanks for committing to help us at our concert. I'm greatly looking forward to St Jude's Day and to welcoming so many people to Forling Down for this wonderful event."

"I'll run you both to Norwich Station," said Colonel Wagstaff to Benedict and Chas. "I've got to do some shopping."

"That's very kind," replied Benedict, "delighted to accept."

With that, the various parties filed out of the church. Ned and Pru kindly did the clearing up; Aubrey jumped onto his bike and made his way to the Newt and Ferret for a 'lemonade' or two; and Cyril, actually quite exhausted by the meeting after all the unnecessary interventions by his least favourite people, made his way slowly across the road to the Rectory.

Lu was left in the church, having decided that perhaps it was an idea to do a little bit of organ practice. It had yet to be decided what part he was to play in the concert.

Chapter 20

How Is It possible to involve Lu?

A few days later, Fr Cyril was woken by the Rectory phone at eight thirty a.m. This was far earlier than he intended to rise as it was one of the days that his curate said Morning Prayer at St Jude's. He rolled his frame out of bed, donned his faded blue dressing gown, and slowly descended the staircase, muttering some unholy expletives as he did!

"Who the blazes needs to phone the Rectory at this ungodly hour?" he whispered.

"Good morning Rector," began the caller, "Gustav Less here, calling from a rainy Munich. I trust all is well in Forling Down and that concert preparations are going well?"

The Rector cleared his throat and adjusted his horn-rimmed spectacles which had been hastily grabbed as he shuffled out of his bedroom. "All fine here Herr Less," stuttered Cyril, trying to come to terms with his rude awakening. "And we had a very productive planning meeting in the church last Saturday morning."

"Excellent," said Gustav. "The purpose of my call is a rather sensitive one, prompted by a conversation that I have just had with Chas Grundy regarding your Director of Music, Mr Pipe. Apparently, and somewhat surprisingly, I gather that his skills are somewhat limited? I think it would be lovely to involve him with the orchestra in some way, but I don't want to embarrass him or put him under undue stress?"

"Chas is absolutely correct in his assessment of Mr Pipe," responded Cyril. "His enthusiasm however is not matched by his keyboard skills I'm afraid, and although I myself am not a musician, I gather from those that are, that he only feels even mildly confident playing in the key of G Major?"

"I see," replied Gustav after quite a pause on the other end of the line. "This could be an interesting challenge but one that I am prepared to face full on! Suppose I transpose 'Abide with me' from its usual key of Eb major up to G Major, then perhaps Mr Pipe would feel confident in joining in with the organ?

"It would be a reflective and moving piece to conclude the concert, and of course very appropriate in a church setting?"

"That sounds a wonderful idea Herr Less, and one that should appeal to Mr Pipe I think. I will have a conversation with him in the next few days and confirm. I do appreciate you being prepared to go to all this trouble for our small Norfolk village."

"It's a pleasure, Rector – happy to help," replied Gustav. "The evening will be a bit of light relief after quite a demanding eight month concert tour throughout Europe. You can always get a message passed to me via Chas Grundy. 'Auf Wiedersehen' for now!"

Cyril fell back in his comfortable chair trying to take stock of all the extraordinary things that were unfolding in his usually quiet country parish. He was beginning to feel rather stressed by the prospect of having to coordinate such a mammoth undertaking – matters seemed to be gaining momentum and Cyril was beginning to feel rather out of control. He eventually decided that he had better do his ablutions and don his clerical clothes and of course.........he had yet to have breakfast.

Half an hour later, Fr Cyril was beginning to feel a bit more confident and positive. He mused that it was amazing what a couple of cups of strong coffee could do! He slowly opened the Rectory door and made his way across the road to the church. Upon arrival, he was greeted by the sound of the organ which was churning out 'Amazing Grace' over and over again rather like a CD on a loop!

"Oh for heaven's sake!" muttered Cyril as he made his way up the aisle to the willowy figure at the console. Needless-to-say it was Lu Pipe doing his utmost to try to improve his facility on the organ. There was just one manual on this ageing country instrument and it had a very limited range of stops. The joke in the congregation was that Lu had three stops, loud, medium and soft! Normally, he favoured the 'loud' option which didn't go down well with the more discerning worshippers!

"Good morning Pipe," bellowed Cyril above the organ blasts. "Please stop for a minute, (or even longer if possible he added under his breath)! I need to discuss a few matters with you about the concert."

Lu visibly jolted upwards on the organ stool, shocked by the stentorian sounds emanating from his Rector. "Oh my," he sighed after a few seconds, "you gave me quite a shock then Rector. I was just doing a bit of practice."

"That's what you call it, is it?" chided the Rector, once again like an old school headmaster. "I've never heard such a cacophony! Now Lu, listen to me very carefully please, I will say this only once," he mocked using a pseudo French accent reminiscent of the BBC series 'Allo, Allo'! "Gustav Less, the conductor of the Munich Radio Orchestra, is being extraordinarily charitable and wants to involve you, and the organ, in a final item in the concert. He has selected the hymn 'Abide with me' and I'm sure you'll be delighted to learn that he is going to ensure that the music will be written in G Major!"

Lu Pipe was quite overcome. A mixture of excitement and trepidation rose through his veins and he began to visibly perspire.

"Well I was hoping to have a little spot," began Lu, "and I thought it would be a very short solo item? But to play alongside the Munich Radio Orchestra under the baton of maestro Herr Less is just beyond my wildest dreams. I can't thank you enough Rector for arranging this. I apologise for all the occasions that I have been grumpy or less than compliant. You are a great Rector and Forling Down is so fortunate to have you as its parish priest."

"That's enough Mr Pipe. I can't take any of the credit for this proposal I'm afraid. It was the suggestion of Mr Less himself, but I have to say it is a most charitable one, and one that should relieve you of a great deal of stress. I am bound to say that it will also minimise any embarrassment that the parish may have from your playing!"

"Well really, now you are spoiling the whole jolly thing Rector," began Lu.

"Just being frank and honest Lu. You must admit that your facility at the keyboard is somewhat limited!" interjected Fr Cyril. "Now I must be off. I suggest you practice 'Abide with me' in the right key once the music arrives from Germany."

The parish organist was left in the church astride the organ stool, red-faced, embarrassed and rather cross, but also just a little bit excited about what the future could hold. Lu Pipe playing the organ with the Munich Radio Orchestra? Was this really happening or was it all a confusing dream? He touched the keys of the organ manual just to make sure it was all real. Then he started practising the scale of G major, over and over again. He was determined to shake off the hurtful opinions of many of the villagers regarding his organ playing once and for all. This was going to be his chance to shine.

Just then, the south door of the church creaked open and St Jude's eccentric curate Fr Aubrey bounded up the centre aisle.

"What ho Lu Pipe!" sniggered Aubrey, "how's your organ doing today?" Although Aubrey cracked this joke with unfailing regularity, he personally always found it hilarious. His snigger developed quickly into loud shrieks and giggles, then further developed into uncontrollable guffaws! Aubrey seemed to have perpetual schoolboy humour despite the fact that he was now in his mid-thirties.

Lu, also with unfailing regularity, was extremely irritated by Aubrey's immature teasing and inevitably rose to the bait!

"The church organ is absolutely fine thank you Mr Crediton-Smythe," began Lu in his usual dismissive manner, "and I'll thank you not to be so smutty. I do not expect to have to endure hurtful innuendo from a man of the cloth of all people."

"Oh man up!" said Aubrey abruptly, still hardly being able to control himself. "You would never have survived Eton!"

"I'm very pleased indeed that I didn't have to endure Eton," continued Lu. "Now if you don't mind, I need to do some organ practice. Just wait until you see me at the concert – I think that silly grin may be wiped off your face once and for all."

Aubrey found that last prospect even more hilarious and gladly disappeared into the vestry to prepare everything for the midday communion service. He and Lu were certainly not bosom buddies but both tolerated each other in small doses! Lu continued his scales for a further ten minutes before deciding to call it a day. He then sought solace in the Newt and Ferret for a lunchtime pint and some much-needed reflection.

Chapter 21

Concert Invitations and Detailed Preparations

During August, life in sleepy Forling Down progressed at its usual slow Norfolk pace, although talk of the up-coming concert was very much on people's lips. Posters had been produced by Mrs Bloomfield-Upton on her home computer and these had been placed all around the village. Edwin Jones, the butcher, had posted one in his shop, as had Cynthia Gumbrel who ran the village store. There were quite a few around, plus A5 flyers in the Newt and Ferret; and of course many in and around St Jude's Church. Colonel Wagstaff had a large poster on the gate to The Manor House and even the local bus from Norwich (Tuesdays only!), carried a poster in the window by its passenger door!

The Colonel had suggested a special PCC meeting to firm up more precise details and this was scheduled for early September, once again in the upper room at the Newt and Ferret.

Such was the growing excitement regarding the concert, there was record attendance at this meeting when, most unusually, every single PCC member was present. As the councillors took their seats, there was an excitable hum of happy discussion, in stark contrast to the usual lethargic murmurings, more the normal feature of these gatherings.

Fr Cyril was last to arrive as usual but once he had negotiated the winding, creaky staircase up to the room, he took his place at the head of the table.

"I think we should start with a prayer of thanks for all our blessings," began the Rector, "so let us pray. *Father, we thank you for all the blessings you bestow upon us, particularly the promise of the church concert coming up next month. We ask for your blessings on our discussions tonight and pray that all our plans may be brought to fruition – Amen*"

"Ow, ow, ow," shrieked Mrs Bloomfield-Upton, who had been inadvertently prodded in the behind by a sharp pencil being retrieved from the floor by Rodney Hitcham! He had lost his balance whilst trying to regain the vertical, and in so doing had sunk his writing implement into the unsuspecting buttock of the PCC Secretary!

"Sorry old thing!" puffed a red faced Rodney as he regained control and the vertical. "Hopefully no lasting damage to the jolly old cheeks Bloomers!"

"I beg your pardon Hitcham," retorted a VERY cross and affronted secretary. "Mrs Bloomfield-Upton is my name, you impudent and impertinent apology for a human being. Didn't they teach you any manners at that public school of yours?"

This was all too much for Aubrey who was desperately trying to stifle giggles by getting out his handkerchief.

"That was a lovely prayer!" said Prudence Pots, one of the village's more simple residents! "I found it rather moving!"

Fr Cyril was getting progressively more red-faced at all these ridiculous distractions and Colonel Wagstaff was staring at the Chair, willing him to get a grip of things sooner rather than later.

There was another thump on the table by the Rector, this time even firmer and louder than before.

"Order, order!" declaimed the Rector.

"Mine's a pint!" whispered Aubrey to Ned Gaskin who was seated on his left side.

"Oh yes, me too!" said Ned. "Oid loik a glass of Abbot ale please!"

"ORDER!" shouted Cyril even louder. "This particularly applies to the more cerebrally challenged members of this motley assembly! Now can we bring some sanity to our meeting as we have much to discuss if this concert is to be a success."

"Hear, hear!" barked the Colonel, who was displaying equal frustration and irritation. "Please keep control Rector – I have another meeting at the Manor in two hours' time and at the present rate of progress, I will have zero chance of getting there!"

The Rector did eventually regain control of the meeting and thankfully important progress was made. It was agreed that Mrs Bloomfield-Upton would send out VIP invitations to the Bishop of Norwich; the Mayor; the Lord Lieutenant of Norfolk; the local Member of Parliament; and of course to the Prime Minister, Sir John Downing, who had magnanimously agreed to play a part in the concert. It was also agreed that the local police would need to be notified regarding security, particularly that of the Prime Minister, and that the local radio stations and press might also wish to further advertise and cover the event.

The meeting ended without further incident and for once, everyone was united in their desire to make this concert the enormous success it promised to be.

Chapter 22

Choir Practice

It was now just two weeks before the concert and Ludevic Pipe, the organist at St Jude's, had arranged a choir practice. This was not a regular event as the choir had been disbanded some months earlier and in any case, was not by any stretch of the imagination, a competent group of musicians, more a motley gathering of disparate country folk, who in the immortal words of Eric Morecambe, 'sang the right notes but not necessarily in the right order!'

It was a Friday evening in mid-October and there was a chill in the air. The practice was due to start at six thirty p.m. and Lu had opened the church early so he could practise 'Abide with Me' on the organ a few times before the others arrived. Regrettably, after attempting the hymn no less than twenty eight times, not once did he manage to play it all through without any wrong notes, despite the transposition into the key of G major by Herr Less. Lu was more than a bit frustrated and was becoming increasingly stressed by the whole affair. He didn't enjoy choir practices because most of the singers were less than complimentary and compliant, and the thought of having to perform in front of a highly critical and knowledgeable audience under the baton of the legendary Herr Less was bringing on yet another of his cold sweats.

First to arrive was Charity Trussup, the Colonel's housekeeper, closely followed by Prudence Pots who also worked part-time at the Manor. Five minutes later Ned Gaskin walked over from the pub, as did Father Aubrey and the irrepressible Rodney Hitcham.

"What ho Lu Pipe!" called out Aubrey in his usual immature manner. "This had better not go on for too long as we're in the middle of a jolly good darts session over the road! Try and keep things simple and brief old boy if you can," he demanded.

Lu Pipe's face turned a deep crimson and his forebodings about the evening were already beginning to materialise. The church door creaked again and in strolled Edwin Jones, the butcher, and Mrs Napier. Belinda Napier had a young daughter Hermione, so was also keen not to be out for too long as it was the children's bedtime in the Napier house.

"I really must duck out at around sevenish," said Belinda. "Hermione is a bit off colour and suffering from a bout of the 'squits'! I really don't want to leave her with my husband indefinitely!"

"The squits?" shrieked Rodney and Aubrey, almost in unison.

"That's putting me off this evening's curry completely!" interjected Aubrey. "Urgh! Please make sure you sit well away from me old girl – I'm not a fan of the squits!"

"'The squits' sounds like a jolly good name for a pop group," giggled Rodney. "Perhaps we should rename the choir?"

"Please would you be kind enough to take your seats ladies and gentlemen," interrupted Lu, desperately trying to bring some order and sanity back to the proceedings. "On your seats you will find the words and music to 'Abide with me' because this is what we have been asked to sing at the big concert."

"Oi don't think that's gonna be much of a show-stoppa!" drawled Ned in his broad Norfolk accent. "Ow abowt a song from one of them London shows, loik 'Les Miserables' or summat loik thart!"

"We have been asked to sing 'Abide with me' by no less than Gustav Less, the conductor of the Munich Radio Orchestra. He wants us to join in with all the musicians at the end of the concert, in a reflective finale." explained Lu, desperately trying to reassure the assembled company that they would not be exposed to any potential ridicule because their sounds would be very much absorbed into a big orchestral sound, generated by over fifty players from the German radio orchestra.

"What's the jolly old point of us spending hours practising then?" quipped Aubrey indignantly. "Bloody waste of time I reckon!"

"I concur," added Rodney, usually joined to Aubrey at the hip! "I vote we sing the old ditty through once quickly, and then we can get back to Friday night in the Newt and Ferret as usual!"

Lu Pipe was not going to be bullied into curtailing choir practice by a couple of public school boys playing to the gallery. "Let's do a few warm-ups," began Lu. "Please stand and shake your bodies around!"

"Lots of bits bouncing around on your body Charity!" quipped Rodney.

"You shouldn't be looking young Rodney!" chided Charity, going red in the face. "Just concentrate on what Lu is asking us to do and keep your eyes to yourself!"

"Just keeping abreast of things!" giggled Rodney, not in the mood for being put down!

"Now let's stay standing and sing a few scales," continued Lu, determined to wrestle back control. He played a 'C' on the organ and the assembled company attempted a scale of C major. Sadly, Lu did not have the skills to accompany on the organ so what should have been an extremely basic exercise, turned out to be a cacophony of awful sounds, moving at different speeds, and finishing at very different times.

"Oh dear!" shouted Lu above the echoes still reverberating around the church.

"I would put it a bit stronger than that old chap," quipped Aubrey, very frustrated at what he regarded as a continuing waste of time. "If we don't start a bit of proper singing very quickly, my agent will be asking for double time!" he added.

"Mine too!" added Rodney.

"And mine," said Belinda. "Please remember that Hermione has the squits!"

"Oh very well," said Lu. "Please pick up your sheets of paper and let's sing through the hymn. I'll play the first four bars."

"That in itself would be a miracle!" quipped Aubrey under his breath.

Lu did hear the ill-natured remark but on this occasion chose to ignore it. He started playing the melody over with his right hand, actually for once playing most of the notes correctly. With an exaggerated nod of the head, Lu attempted to bring the choir in for the first verse. Needless-to-say, this did not happen seamlessly, but once there had been a general convergence and agreement of the speed, the choir did actually manage one verse, finishing ALMOST at the same time.

"Of course, on the day, Herr Less will be conducting and I shall be on the organ!" explained Lu.

"You and your organ!" quipped Aubrey yet again, never tiring from his habitual teasing.

"The less discussion about your jolly old organ, the better!" added Rodney. "We're all being encouraged to go organic, but in your case I would avoid it at all costs!"

"You two are so beastly!" sighed Lu, "I really don't think I deserve this continual verbal bullying, yes it's verbal bullying," he repeated.

"Yes, pipe down!" you two added Belinda Napier, "forgive the pun, Lu. I really must go and see Hermione. God knows what state she might be in now in her condition. I'm afraid my husband is not a nappy specialist, particularly when it might be riddled with the 'squits'!"

Lu thought the moment had definitely come to conclude choir practice. He announced that he would let everyone know the arrangements for the big day and thanked them for their time that evening. He was drained and more than a little anxious. He was however relieved that he'd got through choir practice relatively unscathed.

The 'choristers' gradually made their way down the aisle and out of the south door. Aubrey and Rodney returned to their darts at the pub and the others made their way back home for their dinners and a Friday night in front of the television. Lu would have gone to the Newt and Ferret too, he was certainly in need of a drink, but the thought of being within sight of Aubrey and Rodney for another hour was too much to bear, so he decided to make his way home for some much-needed liquid refreshment behind closed doors!

Chapter 23

The Big Buildup

It was the week before the concert and Colonel Wagstaff had worked hard, using all his contacts and influence to maximise publicity for the concert. Posters had been printed and circulated featuring the names of all the internationally renowned performers, even including a photograph of the Prime Minister Sir John Downing, who had, to everyone's amazement and delight, agreed to say a few words of welcome. Benedict Cussack, from Anglia Television, had contacted his colleagues at Norfolk's local radio stations and there were promises of a mention and coverage from BBC Radio Norfolk, Heart Norfolk Radio and North Norfolk Radio 96.2 FM. There was indeed a real buzz of excitement which the village had rarely experienced before. Everyone was determined that this fund-raising concert was going to be a resounding success.

Fr Cyril was slightly uneasy as he usually liked to be in complete control of everything. He approached his ministry rather like a public school headmaster, expecting everyone to abide by his directives and he had little time for opposition or red tape. As he made his way over to the church on the Saturday before the concert, he was greeted by a car park full of outside broadcast trucks; yards and yards of black cables; and a massive throbbing generator, already creating the necessary power for all the additional broadcast equipment. Inside the church, there were riggers erecting scaffold towers for cameras and twenty lights were suspended from a temporary cross beam over the central aisle. Microphones were dangling from the old wooden beams and a large temporary stage had been erected in the chancel.

Cyril sat in one of the back pews watching the conversion of his ancient country church into a fully-equipped television studio. A few minutes later, a tall man in a black gilet appeared at the south door, carefully stepping over the network of power cables. He was followed by a sound engineer with rolls of coloured tape attached to his belt, busy ensuring that all the cables were safely placed away from the gangways.

"Hello Father!" said the tall gilet-clad man who cheerfully introduced himself.

"Quentin Hillier – I'm the Director for this outside broadcast. I do hope everything is in order? We're trying very hard to ensure that nothing we do spoils your beautiful church. However, as you can see, we need a great deal of technical equipment to cover these events."

"Please carry on with your important work," said Cyril generously. He was becoming increasingly awestruck by the whole unfolding panorama. "If there is anything you need, please do ask – we are so grateful to you all for supporting our humble event."

"Nothing very humble about this event!" quipped Quentin. "You seem to have a star line-up worthy of any top-priced London concert hall! I take my hat off to you – someone must have some extraordinarily good connections?"

"That would be my curate Aubrey Crediton-Smythe," replied Cyril, not usually wishing to thrust his tiresome curate into the limelight! "He was at Eton with a number of influential people, and somehow, I'm still not quite sure how, he has managed to pull in a few favours. Now, hey presto, you have an unbelievable cast of very talented and well-known performers."

"Good for him!" replied Quentin. "There is much in the saying that 'It's not what you know...etc. etc.! Now, if you'll excuse me, I'd better get on with the day job!"

"Don't let me stop you!" said the Rector. "Thank you again."

Seconds later, Ned Gaskin appeared at the door.

"Moind if oi sit with you, Rector?" he drawled, amazed at the scene unfolding before him.

"Yes, I do mind actually, Ned! I'm enjoying a little solitude in my house of prayer, and I'd rather not be disturbed by the village simpleton!"

"Thart's not very Christian, Rector," countered Ned. "Just cos oi don't have all them qualifications what you 'ave, oi still matter as a 'uman bein' do't oi?"

"It's got nothing to do with qualifications, Gaskin!" replied Cyril. "I'm merely wishing to have some peace and quiet, and I'd rather not sit making small talk to you at the moment. Do you have something to say of such vital importance that it cannot wait?"

"Well, actually oi do," continued Ned. "The Colonel 'as asked me to make sure the bogs go in the roit place in the car park?"

"Oh for goodness sake!" spluttered the Rector, getting increasingly riled. "Toilets, Ned, toilets! I'll thank you not to use such coarse language in church. The toilets need to go on the far side of the car park as far away from the main entrance as you can safely manage. Are they here now?"

"Bein' craned in as oi speak!" said Ned. "Oi'll go an' tell 'em where to stick their units. Very sorry to 'ave troubled you, Rector!"

With that he loped off out of the church, somewhat hurt by the curt way he had been spoken to by his parish priest.

Cyril decided that he had seen enough for the time being and didn't wish to be accosted by anyone else for a while. He carefully stepped over the ever-increasing number of large cables and made his way across the road back to the Rectory.

"Time for a large schooner of my finest cream sherry I think," he muttered under his breath, feeling better already at the prospect of a quiet evening at home.

Chapter 24
Concert Day Rehearsals

Over the previous few months, there had been many careful preparations. What had started out as a casual idea of a little village concert, was now morphing into a mega entertainment event, featuring internationally renown musical performances from some of Europe's top stars. It was to be attended by the Prime Minister, Sir John Downing and was to be covered by all the local broadcast and print media.

Fr Cyril hadn't slept much the previous night as everything was whirring around in his head. He was not generally one for seeking the limelight but now he had been thrust right into it. His parish was to be the subject of discussion, and hopefully admiration, throughout East Anglia and beyond.

After undertaking his usual morning ablutions, Cyril settled down to a breakfast of poached eggs on toast accompanied by a freshly prepared cafetière of ground coffee. The coffee successfully cleared his head and after a microsecond of thought, he decided to conclude his repast with some extra slices of toast topped with his favourite thick cut marmalade. The Rector was now ready to take on the world and the day ahead was indeed promising to be one to remember.

Long before Cyril had woken up, there had been much activity at the church. The sound and lighting riggers had arrived long before daybreak and a breakfast wagon was serving a full English breakfast to all the technicians on site. Extra hospitality vehicles were beginning to arrive and these were to be located fairly near the clergy vestry door to allow for easy access to the stage. A full day of sound checks and rehearsals had been carefully planned by Quentin the Director, and police were also beginning to be stationed at strategic points around the village. A police dog was circling St Jude's, checking for anything untoward and it then moved inside. The handler encouraged it to search everywhere for potential hazards that could harm those attending, not least of course, The Prime Minister.

St Jude's church was quite large by English parish church standards, a bit like the famous Blythburgh Church in the neighbouring county of Suffolk. Thankfully it could accommodate about seven hundred people, although the elaborate staging and technical equipment present would probably reduce this number slightly.

The sizable church hall was being prepared for the interval refreshments and, at the Colonel's suggestion, outside caterers had been hired for the day. Tables were being gaily decorated and hundreds of glasses were being polished and laid out in readiness for some chilled Prosecco later in the evening! The hall fridges were bursting with a wonderful array of varied canapés, and every conceivable type of nibble was on offer on all the tables.

Fr Cyril entered the church at about nine thirty that morning. It did feel more like being in a television studio than a house of prayer but nevertheless, he knew that the benefits to his church and parish were going to greatly outweigh the temporary secularisation of his beloved building.

Ludevic Pipe, the church organist, had been asked to appear for a sound check before all the professional musicians arrived at ten o'clock. He tentatively opened the church door soon after Fr Cyril, and cautiously made his way up to the organ, now very effectively illuminated in a soft purple light. Lu switched on the blowers and selected a low volume setting with the swell box closed. He was very nervous and already felt well out of his depth. Was this day going to be the final humiliation? He had always tried very hard to fight his case when others were unkind about his playing capabilities, but today there was going to be no hiding place. The whole of East Anglia was going to bear witness to his limited keyboard skills and this thought was giving him a genuine ache in the pit of his stomach. His hands were also visibly shaking – a feeling he had not experienced so acutely before.

"Mr Pipe?" enquired a man in a black tee shirt and jeans.

"Ye…Yes," stammered Lu., swivelling round quickly on the stool.

The technician adjusted a couple of directional mics and asked Lu to play a few chords so that the Director in the control vehicle outside could set his levels.

"Any chords?" entreated Lu like a nervous child, now more anxious than ever.

"Yes," replied the techy. "No need to play Widor's 'Toccata' – we just need some organ sound for the levels. Any chords will do."

Lu dug deep into his confidence bank, now rather depleted, and played a chord of G major, followed by a chord of D Major, then returning to G Major. The technician received a message on his portable radio enquiring what setting the organ was on? When told it was the lowest, he requested the highest in order to show the range. Lu, duly selected a full organ setting and repeated the three chords as before.

"That's fine," came the voice of the Director over the radio. "Once we have the full orchestra in place, I can adjust levels as necessary. At least I now know the range."

"That's all for now mate," chirped the techie. "By the way, how many are there in your choir and where will they all be sitting?"

Lu explained that the choir of about twelve usually sat in the choir stalls but now, as a large stage had been erected across the whole chancel area, this would not be possible.

"Where shall we stick the church choir?" enquired the techie on the radio once again.

"I'll come into the church to discuss," came back the disembodied voice from the control vehicle. After a few minutes, Quentin Hillier duly arrived at the south door with headphones around his neck. He strode up the central aisle and scratched his head. After a pause, he suggested putting twelve chairs at the back of the stage on some additional raised blocks which could be brought in from a truck outside.

"That should do the trick," he said, "and we can suspend some extra mics from that beam up there." He pointed to a nine hundred year old cross beam high above the altar rail. "They're only singing right at the end aren't they Mr Pipe?"

"Ye…yes," stammered Lu, who was now, to cap it all, desperate for the toilet! "I think I must just pop to the facilities!"

"Relax old boy and take as much time as you need," said Quentin reassuringly. "I think we're done with you until the full rehearsal at two thirty. Please be on the organ stool in plenty of time as we have a very tight schedule."

Lu was now absolutely bursting for the loo, so he literally ran to the one and only church toilet. Much to his dismay, the door was locked as someone else had beat him to it! He turned on his heels and sprinted back through the south door to the temporary toilets outside. In so doing, he collided with Fr Aubrey who was excitedly lolloping up the church path, eager to see how things were progressing in the building. Lu sent Aubrey sprawling between two gravestones, luckily not causing him any harm or injury.

"What the blazes!" puffed Aubrey trying to regain the vertical. "Have you seen a ghost Pipe?"

"Sorry," blurted out Lu, "I'm desperate for the loo."

"You've been desperate for many years!" retorted the shaken curate. "We've been desperate too, wondering how to cope with you!"

Aubrey's last words had fallen on deaf ears as Lu had eventually disappeared into one of the portable toilets in the car park. Aubrey, who was not at all amused, dusted himself down and continued into the church to soak up the atmosphere.

****

It was now one o'clock in the afternoon and rehearsal time was rapidly approaching. Yet another very large truck had arrived at the entrance to the church car park and the police on duty were doing their level best to ensure efficient parking, always mindful of the need for safe access for pedestrians too. This latest articulated lorry to arrive was that of the Munich Radio Orchestra. It contained many of the large instruments, including timpani; chairs, music stands and perspex screens to shield players in front of the brass. It had the orchestra's name emblazoned on the side.

Two coaches then appeared – the first conveying the orchestra players and the second, the band bus of Plectrum Eight – Wayne Grinter's group. Parking was becoming increasingly difficult, and in the end, the coaches were instructed to remain on the road. Luckily it was wide by country standards and police cones were put around the vehicles to ensure the occasional village traffic was safely alerted.

As well as all the activity outside, a steady stream of people began to enter St Jude's itself. Inside, all the additional lighting had been switched on and the stage area looked absolutely magnificent. It had been very beautifully dressed by the local garden centre and was now awash with chrysanthemums and colourful roses, all garnished with gypsophila and local greenery.

Members of the ad hoc church choir were now arriving, and Ludevic Pipe, fresh from some Dutch courage at the Newt and Ferret, made his way up to the organ stool.

At two fifteen, there was a great hubbub outside. Applause could be heard from the gathered throng, and cameras flashed and clicked away as some special visitors were ushered out of their vehicles. Gustav Less had arrived in a chauffeur-driven Mercedes, closely followed by a luxury minibus containing Andy Grinter, Wayne Grinter and Chas Grundy, their agent. The Colonel and Fr Cyril had been waiting at the door ready to greet the principals – both incredulous at the enormity of the occasion unfolding in front of them. They enthusiastically shook hands with each and exchanged warm-hearted pleasantries. None of the visitors wished to tarry too long at the door as the imminent rehearsal was very much on their minds. After appropriate and courteous exchanges, all made their way up to the stage area in the chancel. Plectrum Eight sat themselves in the front pew on the north side for the time being and Herr Less strode up the temporary stage steps to take his place on the conductor's rostrum. As soon as he appeared, the string players tapped their music stands with their bows and there was a ripple of applause from the other seated players.

Just at that moment, Lu Pipe spotted a large spider gradually crawling over the top of his hymn book on the organ's music desk.

"Aaarh!" shrieked Lu at the top of his voice, "Aaaaaaarh!" He then tried to push himself back as far as possible on the organ stool and in so doing, stepped on the pedal board which responded with a very loud bottom C blaring out across the church!

"How kind!" quipped the conductor as the orchestra players became highly amused and somewhat taken aback by the outburst from Lu. "I've received some interesting 'welcomes' in my time, but that was inspired and quite original!"

Lu had now extricated himself from the organ and was cowering by the choir chairs at the back of the orchestra. "The...the...there's a very large spider on my organ," he blurted.

"HA, HA, HA!" shrieked Aubrey and Rodney from the choir area in unison. "A spider on your organ?? Ha! Ha! Ha!"

"Thart's probably the most excitement 'is organ 'as 'ad for many years oi reckon!" drawled Ned. "Surely you aint afrit of a spoider?"

By now, the entire performance area was convulsed and this incident had certainly lightened the mood! Fortunately, one of the tech guys, not afraid of arachnids, clambered up with a disused disposable coffee cup and deftly removed the errant insect, carefully depositing it outside the building. There was warm applause at this courageous act and then everyone quietened down ready for the conductor.

"Guten Tag!" said Herr Less, warmly welcoming everyone in his heavy German accent. "Thank you very much for coming and for lending your support to this worthy cause. I know the Rector and the folk of Forling Down are hugely grateful to each one of us. Now all we have to do is deliver the goods, so let's start with the final item, 'Abide with me'. We can then release the choir and the organist and they can go home. Firstly, Mr Pipe—please would you give a nice loud 'A' on the organ for orchestral tuning?"

Lu was absolutely delighted that for once he had been asked to do something within his capabilities! He confidently depressed the 'A' key on the organ, and the orchestra responded with their usual tuning routine.

"Choir, will you please stand......and don't worry if you seem to be completely overwhelmed with sound just now. Tonight, of course, the whole audience will be joining with you, so the balance will be a great deal better!"

Herr Less raised his baton and a clear downbeat indicated the start. Lu was observing Herr Less through the mirror above the organ console but was not quick-witted enough to marry what he saw with looking back at his music, and then telling his hands what they needed to play. The embarrassing result was that the organ blasted out notes at least two beats later than those of the orchestra resulting in a less than pleasing overall effect. Herr Less, for the first time that day, was showing signs of frustration and mounting irritation. To compound his unhappiness, Quentin was speaking to him through his ear piece from the control truck outside, explaining that something had to be done to rectify the unacceptable situation.

The conductor clapped his hands, tapped the conductor's stand with his baton, and held his arms up to clearly indicate that he wished the players to stop. Last to stop, needless-to-say was Lu on the organ and his fumblings were now more than ever evident. He was now in fact playing an unwanted organ solo!

"Gott im Himmel!" exclaimed Herr Less. "This is a disaster and cannot continue. We must do two things immediately. Mr Pipe, please alter the organ setting to the quietest you can find, and then only play when the voices come in. Is that clear?"

"Ye...Yes!" stammered Lu, "of course your honour!"

Hugely enjoying this exchange were Aubrey and Rodney rocking back on their choir chairs.

"I think Lu thinks he's talking to a judge!" quipped Aubrey.

"He will end up in court if he carries on like this!" retorted Rodney under his breath.

"Now let's try again," demanded Gustav Less. "We have so much material to get through and this was supposed to be the easy bit!"

The baton once again descended and this time, the piece was performed thankfully without incident. Lu Pipe had been blissfully inaudible as were, to a great extent, the village choir!

The rest of the programme was then rehearsed without incident and the orchestra paused for a tea break at four o'clock. At five, Plectrum Eight took to the stage in front of the orchestra with Wayne Grinter singing his latest hit 'I thought you loved me', currently at number three in the charts. With full orchestral backing, this sounded particularly impressive and Gustav's arrangement worked really well. Wayne's father Andy, a crooner finding fame in the early 70s, then sang the classic 'Blue Moon' – ending the rehearsal in fine form at five thirty.

Gustav was now elated and relieved, and back to his positive self. He had little patience with amateur musicians but he had thoroughly enjoyed the latter part of the rehearsal. His unusual collaboration with the Grinters and Plectrum Eight had given him particular pleasure. The musicians made their way into the bell tower where tea and carrot cake were gratefully consumed. What was the main topic of conversation over tea? Yes, you guessed it – Lu Pipe and his legendary organ!

Chapter 25

The Big Moment Arrives

It was now six thirty in the evening. All the performers were relaxing and getting changed in various hospitality vehicles in the church car park. A large Upod satellite truck had also now arrived outside and was ready to beam the concert direct to the Anglia Television studios in Norwich.

Police dogs were doing a final sweep of the church, both inside and out, as everyone waited for the imminent arrival of the Prime Minister. He was due at any minute as a meeting had been arranged between him and Gustav Less for six forty five. Sir John Downing had been asked to do the 'Welcome' at the start of the concert and he would then take his seat in the front row next to the Colonel and Fr Cyril. The Lord Lieutenant had been invited to be a special guest too, but was sadly abroad at the time and unable to attend. There had been an earlier idea of asking Sir John to compère the whole evening, but this had been fairly quickly shelved as it had been deemed too complicated to coordinate. Sir John's advisers had further counselled against him getting too involved with more menial activities, thought not to be appropriate to the office of Prime Minister.

Crowds were starting to gather outside the church, all eager to see the Prime Minister and his entourage. As the church clock chimed a quarter to seven, two black Range Rovers, preceded by two police motorcyclists, could be seen approaching from the southern end of the village. Cameras flashed and a sole TV Camera filmed the scene as the British Prime Minister arrived to make his first visit to the small sleepy village of Forling Down. A police drone was also keeping a watchful eye overhead.

"Bloody 'ell!" shouted Ned to Prudence who were both on duty at the church lychgate. "Down't think we've 'ad anyone this famous in Forlin' Down since Boadicea's toim! Fancy Sir John comin' to little ole Forlin' Down – oi can't believe it!"

"It's so exciting!" clapped Prudence. "I can hardly contain myself! I haven't felt this excited since seeing Cliff Richard and the Shadows at the Spa Pavilion in Felixstowe over forty years ago!"

"You'd betta contain yerself Prud – there's lots a bobbies abowt tonoit!"

The motorcade swept into the church car park, heralded by cheers and union jack flag waving from the crowd. A plain-clothed detective leapt out of the front passenger seat of the leading car and opened the nearside passenger door. A beaming Sir John Downing emerged, enthusiastically waving at the admiring villagers who were now cheering even louder!

"This sort of welcome is always bloody good for morale!" whispered a beaming Sir John to the detective. "Now which way am I supposed to be going? There should be Herr Less somewhere?"

Gustav Less was waiting nearby outside the plushest of the hospitality vehicles.

"Ah yes, I see him now!" said Sir John, eagerly striding over to see his old acquaintance. "Really good to see you again old boy – how many years has it been?"

"Probably about forty!" answered Gustav, "Very happy memories of the 1970s!"

Gustav Less had not been at Eton but he had been part of the university set who used to get together to enjoy musical and drama productions in the heady days of the 1970s. Sir John had been more involved in the drama side of things and Gustav of course with the music. The two slapped each other firmly on the back and climbed into the relative luxury of the mobile Green Room.

Ned and Prudence made their way up the church path to the south door. Their next task was to check tickets and to show the audience where to sit. They were expecting a full house and eager punters were already filing up the path. As the concert had been well trailed and advertised, a number of coaches had also started to arrive. They were being ushered into the large pub car park opposite which had been commandeered for the evening. Cars had been allowed to park in a large field off the drive up to the Manor House and it was a blessing that the weather was relatively warm and dry – not always the case in Norfolk in late October!

The Colonel and Fr Cyril were in the church early checking that everything was in order. They hovered near the south door ready to usher any VIPs to their reserved seats at the front. The church clock struck seven. There were now just thirty minutes until the start of the most extraordinary event that Forling Down had ever witnessed.

There had been a very large centre-page spread in the previous week's edition of the Eastern Daily Press which related the incredible story of the concert, from its inception to what was rapidly becoming a reality. There had been colour photographs of all the key participants with accompanying mini biographies, and Anglia Television's local news the previous evening had devoted eighty percent of its programme to the concert at St Jude's. Fr Cyril had been interviewed in the church and was now becoming quite a local celebrity, even more famous for a while than the Bishop of Norwich!

At about seven twenty, the Bishop and the Archdeacon arrived and were duly ushered to their seats. The members of the church choir had entered through the vestry door and were now taking their places on the chairs at the back of the orchestra. Rodney and Aubrey were as usual like excitable schoolboys and busy taking photos with their mobile phones.

At seven twenty three precisely, The Prime Minister entered the church flanked by two special protection officers.

"Thought there might be a flourish from some fanfare trumpets!" quipped Sir John as he strode up the centre aisle to take his place.

He was buoyed by enthusiastic applause however which he acknowledged with an enthusiastic wave. Before he took his seat, he warmly shook hands with the other VIPS in the front row and then carefully scrutinised his programme which he found on his seat. As the lights began to dim, he retrieved a sheaf of papers from his inside pocket and checked that he was suitably prepared for his welcome speech.

At seven twenty eight precisely, the orchestra started filing in, taking their places on the especially erected stage. This was to be a bit of light relief for them – not tonight the usual pressures of a performance in a large prestigious concert hall. There followed the usual tuning sounds typical of a symphony orchestra preparing for a concert and there was a hum of excited expectation from the large supportive audience.

At seven thirty, the Leader of the Orchestra, Gurter Payne strode confidently up the steps to the stage and took his customary applause. As the clapping gradually ceased, an eerie calm pervaded the church. The Bishop had been asked to say a short prayer at the start of the proceedings so, at a signal from the floor manager wearing headphones, he made his way up to the pulpit where there was a microphone ready.

"Good evening everyone," began the Bishop, "and welcome to this very special occasion. Before we start, I would like to congratulate Fr Cyril and his team at St Jude's on organising this quite extraordinary event. In all my years of ministry, and certainly in my years as a bishop, I have never known of a small country parish church managing to attempt anything quite so ambitious and uplifting. This determination and resolve should be admired and acknowledged, and I sincerely hope that this evening's performance secures the funds that we know will continue to further God's work in this place. Now let us pray."

The Bishop blessed everyone present, particularly thanking the performers for donating their services, and he gave thanks on behalf of the audience for all their skills and generosity of spirit.

As he resumed his seat, the TV floor manager signalled to the Prime Minister that it was his cue to rise and greet the assembled company.

"Good evening everyone," began Sir John, sweeping back a mop of blond hair as he did so. "You may wonder how it is that a British Prime Minister stands before you in a small rural Norfolk village, beautiful though it is, to lend support to what many may feel is very much a local parochial event. Well, it is indeed local and it is indeed parochial but I believe that special friendships should endure, and it is for this reason that you see me here in Forling Down tonight. I don't think it is any secret that I was at school with a couple of bounders from this parish, no names, no pack drill, and they are seated at the back over there! You know who you are, and I shall be watching you like a hawk! Joking apart, I owe them a big favour, and tonight I am repaying that favour with great pleasure. I have always loved music and I have quite eclectic taste, so I am very much looking forward to the varied programme prepared for us tonight. Now it is my great pleasure to welcome our conductor for this evening, my good friend – Herr Gustav Less!"

There was a crescendo of applause both to thank the Prime Minister for his kind words and to welcome the internationally renowned conductor. Once on the podium, Gustav shook the Leader's hand and asked all the performers to stand to acknowledge their welcome applause too. As the clapping began to die down, the orchestra and choir resumed their seats and the baton was raised to start the programme.

Suddenly there was a high pitched shriek from Prudence Potts at the south door.

"Seagull in the church! ... Seagull in the church! ....Seagull in the church!" she yelled, louder and louder, and higher and higher each time the phrase was uttered!

"Oh Bloody Hell!" muttered Cyril from the front pew, hoping the ground would swallow him up! "What the blazes is going on now?"

Before the south door had been closed for the concert, a wayward gull had indeed flown into the church and was now clearly going to cause much consternation and disruption to the much-awaited proceedings. It flew over the audience a number of times causing a great deal of disquiet. A large aromatic deposit landed on the head of Mrs Bloomfield-Upton who consequently complained very loudly! Then, on a return flight, past, it dive-bombed Pricilla Grindthorpe, dropping more unpleasant matter on a perm she had created at considerable expense just a few hours earlier!

The seagull was becoming increasingly disorientated and for a few moments decided to rest on one of the cross beams over the orchestra, sending a great deal of dust slowly floating down like poppies at the Royal Albert Hall during the Festival of Remembrance. A number of the orchestral players began choking, muttering and then hastily starting to dust and clean their instruments.

Fr. Aubrey thought this could be his moment to shine and therefore raced forward from his position in the choir. He wasn't going to allow a mere bird to spoil all that he had managed to achieve in preparation for this event. As it happened, he had brought a ham sandwich with him hidden in his dinner jacket pocket. He was planning to surreptitiously consume this in a quiet moment at some point during the concert. His devious plan was to attract the gull with some food and tempt it out of the church that way. Startled by Aubrey's charge forward, the gull launched itself once again, bringing down yet more dust and years of decayed matter onto the anxious and increasingly terrified players. It flew around the church another three times before spotting Aubrey's sandwich, now held aloft in front of the brass players. The greedy gull zoomed down but sadly misjudged the sandwich and became firmly lodged in the bell of a euphonium!

"You ridiculous beast." yelled Aubrey, trying not to show any fear. "I think I have you now!" Instinctively, he bent over, ripping the seam of the back of his trousers as he did so, now revealing a rather splendid pair of union jack boxer shorts! Undeterred, he plunged his hand into the bell of the euphonium, and extracted the dazed bird by its legs.

The mood of the audience and performers instantly changed. There was great hilarity at the revelation of Aubrey's underwear and now huge relief that the avian interloper had been apprehended!

Aubrey savoured the moment and held the gull aloft. The audience broke into appreciative applause as he strode down the centre aisle beaming from ear to ear! He could not have been filled with more pride if he had just won the hundred metres! Prudence tentatively opened the south door, hugely relieved, and Aubrey released the stunned bird into the evening air outside the church. As he returned, the orchestral players, now amused rather than dismayed, broke into a chorus of 'For he's a jolly good fellow' much to Aubrey's delight and amusement.

"Bravo Aubrey!" called out Cyril in an unusual burst of curate appreciation!

"No shortage of excitement in rural Norfolk tonight," whispered Sir John Downing to the Bishop. "That curate will go far!"

As Aubrey resumed his position in the choir and the audience settled, Herr Less raised his baton for the second time and the music of Handel's majestic 'Arrival of the Queen of Sheba' floated out across the church, played beautifully by the Munich Radio Orchestra. There then followed Elgar's 'Cello Concerto; a new orchestral composition by Jonathan Willcocks; and the first half concluded with Vaughan Williams' 'Variations on a Theme by Thomas Tallis'.

As the first half concluded, it was now Fr Cyril's turn to clamber up to the pulpit, a task he always found challenging due to his girth and poor level of fitness! Once installed, he cast his eyes over the hundreds of faces before him, dreaming for a moment that this number had come for his morning Sunday service! Rapidly regaining reality, Cyril explained all the interval arrangements and most importantly, the toilet arrangements.

"As numbers are so encouragingly large, we shall have an extended interval tonight of thirty minutes – I think we all need it!" the Rector announced. "Now please do make your way into the church hall where drinks and canapés are now being served."

Cyril clambered down the pulpit steps and the performers repaired to their respective hospitality bases. The VIPs were ushered into the large clergy vestry for their interval fare, partly for security reasons but also to avoid being caught up in the audience crush. Sir John soon became locked in conversation with the Bishop of Norwich, and the

Colonel and Fr Cyril held court with the other specially invited guests.

After thirty minutes had elapsed, Prudence circled around the hall, nave and church car park clanging a large noisy bell. This had been borrowed for the evening from the local village school and was certainly very audible! Gradually the appreciative audience returned to their seats and there was a real buzz of expectation and excitement as they anticipated the very different second half. In great contrast to the first, it was to feature Wayne Grinter and Plectrum Eight; famous ballad singer Andy Grinter, Wayne's father; and the full Munich Radio Orchestra, conducted by maestro Herr Gustav Less. At the conclusion of the concert, also to be thrown into the mix, would be the St Jude's Parish Church Choir and resident organist, Ludevic Pipe! What was there not to like?

All the performers had reclaimed their seats, and all the extra equipment required for the singers and band had been installed on the stage by the technical crew during the interval. Suddenly, amidst a sudden plume of dry ice and some on-stage pyrotechnics, Wayne Grinter appeared, running up the full length of the central aisle of the church. With great dramatic effect, he leapt onto the stage, grabbed a microphone, and Plectrum Eight immediately began playing the introduction to their first song. More dry ice then filled the front of the stage and the audience was treated to thirty minutes of many of Wayne Grinter's hits from the previous decade. A special orchestral arrangement had been added to the last song, 'Will I see you again?' and the whole church was filled with the most uplifting and emotional musical swell of sound. Not only was all this being thoroughly appreciated by the church audience, it was also being simultaneously beamed to the whole of East Anglia via satellite link too. If all this was not enough, as the applause began to die down, Andy Grinter appeared through the fog of the dry ice to join his son for a very special final offering – the classic balled 'Blue Moon'. As the famous father and son duetted, the ethereal strings of the orchestra soared above the sound of the band, and a number in the audience were seen to have tears running down their cheeks. Couples were holding hands and even the Prime Minister, normally a bit of a tough guy, was observed extracting a handkerchief from his pocket to wipe away an emotional tear. This concert in a small Norfolk country village was now rivalling the best given by André Rieu and his Johann Strauss Orchestra! As the last notes floated up to the church roof and the Grinters hugged each other on stage, the audience erupted into enthusiastic applause and admiration – all rising to their feet to further show their warmest appreciation.

As the applause and raw emotion eventually died down, Gustav Less turned to speak from the microphone located behind his podium.

"Thank you Forling Down for giving us such an amazing ovation," began Gustav. "When I agreed to take part in this concert, I wasn't sure if I had made a huge error of judgement! Well I now know that I did make the right judgement and I sincerely hope that our efforts this evening have, in some small way, helped to support the work of this beautiful church in this lovely English village." As he paused, the applause began again. "We are now going to conclude our evening's programme with the very moving and reflective hymn 'Abide with Me' which of course asks our God to be with us always. I am delighted that we shall be joined by the choir of St Jude's and the church's resident organist Mr Ludevic Pipe!"

There was a ripple of polite applause and some amused exchanges of anxious glances from those 'in the know' in the village! How could Lu Pipe and the ad hoc church choir, possibly compare with the professionalism and talent already enjoyed on the stage? Well only time would tell! Gustav asked the audience and choir to stand. He turned back towards the orchestra and caught Lu's eye in the organ mirror! Lu adjusted his position nervously on the organ stool and once again made the classic error of stepping on one of the notes on the pedal board with his left foot! A loud bottom 'A' rang out across the church and the audience started to chuckle. Gustav by this time was beyond being professionally offended, so turned to the audience to explain that the organ was 'just tuning up'! At this well-timed quip, there was yet more laughing and actually a crescendo of applause too! Gustav turned back, raised his baton and the orchestra began playing the introductory four bars. Lu had written himself a large note which he had stuck on the organ which said 'Only play when the singers come in'! Fortunately he heeded this advice and, as the organ was thankfully on a fairly quiet setting, it was mercifully almost inaudible given the rich and glorious sound coming from the orchestra. The Grinters and Plectrum Eight, still on the stage, joined in with the singing too, and as the third verse drew to a close, Gustav indicated a big closing rallentando which brought the very memorable evening to a close. Still standing, the audience clapped even louder and some even stamped their feet. Gustav acknowledged the applause and shook the Leader's hand. He then swept off the stage, encouraging the Grinters to follow him. As the applause continued, willing the stars to reappear, Gustav pushed Andy and Wayne back on to take their own personal applause. Gustav then strode back on, shook hands with the Grinters and invited all the performers to stand and acknowledge the audience's appreciation.

At this point, Sir John Downing felt a deep urge to say a few words, so he moved from his seat and climbed up into the pulpit. He indicated to the audience to sit down and the orchestra and choir did likewise.

"Don't worry!" he began, "I'm not going to preach a sermon!"

At this, the audience laughed and applauded loudly. Sir John beamed, again sweeping back his characteristically untidy blond hair with his right hand!

"I just could not let this evening pass without saying a few words on behalf of us all. We have been treated to the most amazing feast of music tonight, delivered by some of the most talented musicians in Europe, or dare I say, the world. Performers…I know you have all donated your services this evening which is no small gesture, and we all sincerely thank you and salute you!"

As he paused, there was yet more applause. He had certainly captured the feelings and mood of everyone present.

"I think also, particular thanks should go to our resident musicians, Mr Pipe and his church choir. It takes guts to join forces with seasoned professionals and you have done so with good humour and great energy. What you may lack in talent, you have certainly made up for in enthusiasm! If I may say so Mr Pipe, your bottom 'A' on the organ before 'Abide with me' was a particular highlight for me!"

At this, there was raucous laughter and yet more polite applause.

"Now I must finish as it is getting late, but let's show our appreciation once more for all these wonderful musicians who, through their talent and generosity of spirit, have given us a fantastic evening's entertainment. God bless you all and have a safe journey home!"

With this, the audience rose to their feet once again and clapped even more loudly, this time for a full four minutes. As the ovation began to wane, the Colonel and Fr Cyril escorted the Prime Minister down the aisle, acknowledging greetings as he went. The conductor, Leader and performers then filed out through the vestry entrance, and the audience spilled out of the south door, so grateful that they had been privileged to witness such a memorable evening.

"Fancy a nightcap up at the Manor?" whispered the Colonel to Cyril as they watched the Prime Minister's motorcade disappear into the distance.

"That would be very much appreciated," said Cyril as the pair made their way up the nearby drive to the Manor House.

An hour and two large ports later, Fr Cyril retraced his steps down the Manor drive and across the road opposite the church to the Rectory. He slumped into his favourite chair and gave a deep sigh. Today had been a good day – a very good day indeed!

Chapter 26

The Aftermath and Postscript

The next morning, the Rectory phone rang very early at seven thirty. Cyril was not at all ready to rise and he was not best pleased at this rude awakening. He tossed and turned, putting the pillow over his head to deaden the sound, but eventually gave in and staggered out of bed. He fumbled for his dressing gown, very bleary-eyed, and shuffled his way slowly down the stairs. He angrily picked up the receiver and sharply announced – "The Rectory!"

"Good morning Rector," began a voice at the other end of the line. "My name is Freddi Ricardo – I am one of the Producers of the BBC 'Look East' programme. I have been reliably informed that your church mounted a particularly newsworthy concert last night and I have been forwarded some of ITV's footage which looks absolutely incredible? I'm calling to ask if you would consider doing an interview with one of our reporters for this evening's programme?"

Fr. Cyril was trying hard to quickly absorb all this information as he had yet to properly wake up. He was certainly not in a position to receive guests from the media!

"I'm afraid you have caught me at a rather inconvenient moment," began the Rector! "What time are you suggesting that a reporter might appear?"

"Well," began Mr Ricardo, "this can be entirely at your convenience. Would late morning, say eleven thirty, be a possibility? This will give our team time to edit the interview and prepare it for the programme this evening?"

Cyril cleared his throat and quickly tried to mentally map out his day.

"Yes, I think that could work," he stuttered. "May I suggest your reporter meets me inside St Jude's Church?"

"Fantastic Rector – thank you!" replied Freddi, "I'll make sure our reporter is with you then and congratulations on what was clearly an amazing event."

"Goodbye," said Cyril sharply, noting down the agreed time in his diary on the table by the phone.

He then shuffled back up the stairs and started to run a bath. Once filled, and with an inviting steam forming over it, he turned off the taps and started to remove his purple pyjamas. He glanced in the mirror as he did so and as usual mentally agreed that this was not a pretty sight! He quickly averted his eyes once again and dipped his left foot into the water to test the temperature. Then.........the Rectory phone rang again!

"Oh for Heaven's sake!" shouted Cyril in a very exasperated tone. "What on the earth is it now?"

He dried his foot on the bath mat, quickly wrapped his dressing gown around his rotund frame, and once again made his way down the Rectory stairs to the phone in the hall.

"The Rectory!" he shouted again, even more abruptly than before.

"Ah, good morning Rector!" began a voice at the other end. "My name is Conrad Blunt and I am from the Daily Mail in London. I gather you had a rather splendid concert in your village last night? I wonder if you would allow us to send a reporter and a photographer up to Forling Down sometime this afternoon? We could be with you at about two thirty?"

Cyril again cleared his throat, peered at his diary without his spectacles on and replied "Oh very well! Please come to St Jude's Church and meet me there."

"Thank you," replied Conrad, "You sound a bit hassled Rector?"

"Well I won't bore you with the details," replied Cyril, "but I was about to get into what WAS a hot bath! I fear that it might be rather lukewarm by now!"

"Oh, I'm so sorry," apologised Conrad. "I'll leave you to it now and hopefully I won't have chilled your water too much? Cherio for now!"

"Er, goodbye," responded Cyril curtly, once again noting down the time in his diary.

He made his way back up the stairs yet again, flung his dressing gown over a chair and at last immersed himself in the relaxing waters of the bath. Remarkably it was still pretty hot and was one of Cyril's treasured safe spaces.

After a few moments, yes you guessed it, the phone rang yet again!

"I don't believe it!" bellowed Cyril at the top of his voice, sounding and resembling a pained hippopotamus. The sound was so loud, it echoed around the walls of the large Rectory bathroom.

"Whoever it is this time can just hang on. Go talk to Beelzebub, and if needs be, try again later!"

The phone rang for a full five minutes but Cyril stoically resisted its beckoning and was determined to complete his ablutions without further disturbance.

It transpired that the last caller was Priscilla Grindthorpe, the church treasurer. She was desperate to share the good news that the concert had raised a magnificent fifty thousand pounds. She phoned again an hour later, suspecting that the Rector may have been temporarily indisposed.

"That is quite wonderful!" said Cyril. "Who would have thought that sleepy old Forling Down could raise such a magnificent amount? Do bank it straight away please Priscilla and make sure that you take someone with you."

"All is well Rector," said Priscilla. "The Colonel has offered to take me in his car this afternoon."

"Excellent," responded Cyril, "we shall have some very good news to impart to the PCC next week and I shall share this news with the world at large when I am interviewed by the press later today."

$$* * * * * * * * * * * * * *$$

The concert had indeed been a huge success and the church's finances were considerably more secure. Remarkably, the concert had not only brought a degree of fame to this previously unremarkable Norfolk village, but it had also drawn the villagers closer together. Rarely now would there be unkindness, teasing or squabbling. Ludevic

Pipe had gone from being an object of persistent ridicule to somewhat of a hero. The church organ was to be upgraded and tuned, making it much more pleasing to the ear, and the PCC had formally congratulated and applauded Fr Aubrey and his friend Rodney on their contribution to the concert, not least for making it possible to involve the Prime Minister. It had further been resolved that there should be a special party and church service each succeeding year in order to celebrate St Jude's Day.

Fr Cyril's reputation with the Bishop of Norwich had been transformed and previous irritations and long-held grudges had evaporated. He was, against all expectation, promoted to be the next Archdeacon of Norfolk.

St Jude, also known as Judas Thaddaeus, was one of the Twelve Apostles of Jesus and he had certainly worked his spiritual magic on Forling Down. Once a community of bickering and ridicule, this Norfolk village had now become a beacon of hope and inspiration.

"God bless St Jude and God bless Forling Down," said Fr Cyril as he prepared for his bed. "For many years, I had lived in a limbo of despair and frustration. Now, St Jude, you have shown me the way – thank you!"

The End